It was a cold, cheerless room with bars covering the single window through which filtered a grey dusty light. A clock ticked somewhere, and the sounds of the world outside were muted. Patricia and her lawyer faced each other across a table. The police guard was discreetly out of earshot, but attentive all the same. 'The truth is, I didn't do it,' Patricia said with some emotion, but still keeping her voice low. 'I'm not the sort of woman who hits people over the head with a bottle of Scotch . . .'

SONS AND DAUGHTERS 4

Carl Ruhen

From an idea by Reg Watson and based on the scripts of John Alsop, Dan Battye, Colin Bowles, Ian Coughlan, Ysabelle Dean, Steve Dunne, Greg Haddrick, Ray Kolle, Bevan Lee, Maureen Ann Moran, David O'Brien, Peter Pinne, Betty Quin, Stuart Ray, Jane Seaborn, Greg Stevens, Rod Weaver, Alister Webb, and Anthony Wheeler.

A STAR BOOK
published by
the Paperback Division of
W.H. Allen & Co. Plc

A Star Book
Published in 1986
by the Paperback Division of
W.H. Allen & Co. Plc
44 Hill Street, London W1X 8LB

First published in Australia as a QB Book by Horwitz
Grahame Books Pty Ltd, 1986

Copyright © Horwitz Grahame Books Pty Ltd, 1986

Printed and bound in Great Britain by
Anchor Brendon Ltd, Tiptree, Colchester, Essex

ISBN 0 352 31987 9

SONS AND DAUGHTERS 4

ONE

Sitting in a police cell was not Patricia's style at all. The fact that she was there on a murder charge made it even less of a joy.

If the evidence against her when she was first arrested was circumstantial, there was now something more positive to go on. As Ted Burns, her solicitor, told her that afternoon in the police interview room, it looked as if they were facing an uphill battle. For one thing – and this was aside from the motive, which, while strong enough, could nevertheless be fought with some confidence – there was the evidence of the traces of skin that had been found under her fingernails, which meant that she had been lying about having stayed home that night. She had seen Luke Carlyle, and had got into a fight with him. It looked bad. In fact, the odds couldn't have been more stacked against her.

'Whose side are you on?' Patricia demanded

sullenly. 'You're supposed to be *defending* me, not prosecuting.'

The lawyer was a small and patient man. He spoke calmly. 'I'm simply trying to get to the truth,' he pointed out.

It was a cold, cheerless room with bars covering the single window through which filtered a grey dusty light. A clock ticked somewhere, and the sounds of the world outside were muted. They faced each other across a table. The police guard was discreetly out of earshot, but attentive all the same. 'The truth is, I didn't do it,' Patricia said with some emotion, but still keeping her voice low. 'I'm not the sort of woman who hits people over the head with a bottle of Scotch.'

Nor was she the sort of woman who would be able to endure being locked up in a police cell for much longer, listening to voices and the echoing clang of steel doors. Burns said, 'You realise of course that your friend, Mrs Bartlett, will now have no choice but to testify against you?'

Charlie . . . Patricia sighed. Even Charlie Bartlett was believing that Patricia was guilty of murder which was a very nice thing for one's best friend to believe. It was a comforting thought to have while sitting it out in a police cell facing a future which, to say the least, looked very bleak. When the police had first come to question her about the murder, Charlie had

8

agreed that Patricia had not left the house that night, but it was obvious that she hadn't been too happy about it. Then Charlie had begun to have twinges about not having told the complete truth about Patricia's movements, and when she had been questioned again . . . Damn, Charlie! If only Charlie hadn't been anxiously waiting up for her, knowing the mood she had been in, when she had returned from Luke's flat at some time after midnight. 'Thank you for cheering me up,' Patricia said drily.

The lawyer replaced the papers in his brief-case. 'You know you can always find yourself another solicitor if you're not happy with me,' he remarked, a cold edge creeping into his voice.

Patricia felt the warmth rush up into her face. Perhaps she had gone too far. Everything was happening at once; the tension was unbearable. 'I'm sorry,' she said quietly. 'It's just that it's so unfair.' Her hands were tightly clasped together. Her lower lip trembled slightly. 'I'm innocent, you see. I didn't kill Luke Carlyle.'

Her fingernails had raked the side of his face, leaving a vivid and angry mark. They had found skin under her fingernails, which, put together with the strongest possible motive she had for killing the man who had calmly and systemati-cally set out to ruin her, made her the obvious suspect. When they had first questioned her about the murder, she had thought, with

Charlie's help, she had established an alibi for the time he was said to have been killed. Then, a short time later, to her dismay, they had come back just as she was about to leave the house with her packed bags and placed her under arrest.

Burns nodded. 'Fine. I accept that. But you must put me completely in the picture.' He stared at her mildly. A telephone was ringing in another room. 'As the case stands at the moment,' he continued as the ringing stopped, 'it will look very cut and dried to a jury. We've got to come up with something – anything that can throw reasonable doubt on the prosecution's evidence.'

'I understand,' Patricia murmured as he closed his briefcase and rose to his feet. She looked up at him hopefully, although she didn't really feel there was cause for hope. But she had to try, to grasp out for anything she could. 'Could you do something for me?' she asked.

The policeman at the other end of the room was also standing. 'As your legal representative,' Burns said, 'I'll be doing everything possible for you.'

'No . . . it's personal.' David was still angry with her. She had humiliated him, and he had told her that there was no way he would allow her to make a fool of him ever again. She had needed his help, had pleaded with him to forgive her, sell the house and start over again in some

10

place where no one knew them, but he had refused. She had hurt him badly. He had been very bitter – and perhaps he had good reason. After all, Patricia had called the wedding off at the very last minute, in front of all the guests, in front of the marriage celebrant, with David standing at her side and the smell of roses filling the room, and while a video camera recorded every precious moment. 'I would like you to get in touch with a friend of mine – David Palmer.'

She had tried to explain to David why she had run away, fear-stricken, leaving them all standing there, staring after her in amazement. But he hadn't understood. Burns took a notepad from his briefcase and a pen from his pocket. 'Does he have a phone number?'

Patricia shook her head. There was no telephone at the ramshackle old place David had bought out at Sunbury, and on which he spent most of his free time working to make habitable. They had had plans for that house. 'You'll have to drive out and see him,' she said. She had driven out there herself that morning, but it had been a waste of time. But that was just before Luke Carlyle's body had been discovered in his flat among the broken pieces of the Scotch bottle that had been smashed over his head. That was before she had been charged with Luke's murder. As if it wasn't already bad enough to learn on her wedding day that she had been cleaned

11

out, ruined by a man she had trusted.

'All right.' The lawyer pushed the pad and pen across the table. 'Write down the address.' Patricia began to write. 'Will Mister Palmer be able to help us?'

She had told David she still loved him, but it wasn't the same as when they had run away all those years ago – and how much had happened since that time, the kids grown up, marriages and breakdowns, births and deaths, triumphs and defeats – and they had been kids themselves, and the future had looked deceptively bright enough. But now . . . . to become legally involved with him again . . . well, it wouldn't really be any different from what it had been before. Thanks to Luke Carlyle she was broke. It was all right to think about marriage when she had something behind her, but the thought of having to survive – which was exactly what it would be – on David's salary was just too awful to consider. As she had told him that day, she needed money – that was the way she was, and to be perfectly honest with him she couldn't pretend to either him or herself that she would be happy just getting along like most other people. He must see, she had persisted in the face of his bitterness, that it was because she loved him that she was breaking it off now, and not later. 'You can justify it any way you like, Pat,' David had retorted angrily before storming out of her bedroom, 'but all I know is that you've made me look a prize idiot – and believe me, that's the last time you'll ever do it.' She had watched him go with tears welling in her eyes.

'No.' Patricia slid the pad and pen back across the table. 'But he's a . . . close friend. I was hoping he would get in touch.' She smiled wanly; she was feeling utterly miserable and alone, and wished she didn't feel so doubtful of David's support. 'I suppose he hasn't heard yet. Please . . .' she looked imploringly up at Burns . . . 'just tell him what has happened. He'll realise it's all a terrible mistake: I can always rely on David when I need him.' Her lip was trembling again; the tears were not far away. 'And God, I do need him now,' she whispered.

Back in her cell, surrounded by ominous echoes and while she waited to hear the results of the lawyer's visit to David, either from him or, hopefully, from David himself, she had plenty of time to think about the events that had led to the predicament in which she now found herself. It was hard to believe it had all happened in such a short space of time.

A wedding present, Luke Carlyle had told her; he had come to the house that day to give her a wedding present, and she had been pleased to think he should have gone to the trouble. 'You shouldn't have done that,' she had said happily. Her wedding day; she had been like a young girl; an old love, a new setting, and it should have been the happiest day of her life. And it had been until that moment he had handed her the file he was holding and told her it was a list of the company assets – or what *had* been the company assets, because they no longer existed, no assets, no shares, no cash reserves, even the clients' money had gone, all of it converted to cash and transferred out of the country. He had destroyed her company – that was his wedding present. Patricia shuddered when she recalled the sensation of coldness and weakness she had experienced when her puzzlement was replaced by the awful import of what he was telling her.

Luke had mentioned his father – something about his father appreciating the irony of the situation because Luke would be using a great deal of his father's money to escape from him once and for all – and then it all began to fall into place. In some way or another, he had found out about Patricia's partnership with Roger Carlyle, and this was his revenge for being duped into believing that it was purely on his own merits that Patricia had taken him into the company, had handed him so much responsibility, when in fact his father had been behind her all the time, being his own sweet manipulative self, putting up the money, making conditions, spreading his tentacles over the son who had already travelled from one side of the continent to the other to escape an influence he found to be intolerable.

But his father had followed him. His father had wanted him back. And now Luke was dead, and as soon as father learnt that Patricia had been charged with his murder . . . Patricia shuddered again. He would stop at nothing to get back at her . . . an eye for an eye. She knew how ruthless Roger Carlyle could be.

Luke had warned her that Roger would not allow her to call the police and have him arrested as the common criminal she had accused him of being. He would not appreciate becoming a laughing stock when it was learnt he had been fleeced by his own son. He would make a song and dance about what had happened, sure, but if Patricia brought the police into it, if the whole matter became public, Roger Carlyle would have her for breakfast, and despite herself, Patricia conceded he might have had a point.

She paced impatiently up and down the length of her cell, back and forth, her arms folded, her forehead creased in thought, waiting to hear back from either the solicitor or David – waiting to hear something. Burns had told her that she would be held in custody for the remainder of the weekend before being brought before a magistrate on Monday morning. Bail would be set, something in the vicinity of two thousand dollars, he guessed, if she could find someone to stand guarantor for her. But the more she thought about it, the more she realised, like it or not, that she would really be much safer if she remained in jail until she was proven innocent of Luke's murder. Outside, Roger Carlyle would be waiting for her – Roger, or someone hired by him . . .

When she had called him in Perth to let him know what his charming son had done to them both, Roger's reaction was blunt and uncompromising. No police, he had commanded. If she went to the police, as she had just threatened to do, he had promised her it would be the sorriest day of her life. If the matter became public he had threatened to make it look as if it were Patricia herself who had defrauded the company while using his son to cover her tracks. Patricia had been appalled. Did he really mean he was just going to sit there and do nothing while his son robbed him blind? Roger had snapped that it was none of her business what he did. His voice had been steely; Patricia had struggled to keep her own level. Even after she had refunded half the money belonging to her clients, with Roger putting up the other half as had been stipulated in their agreement, she was still going to be left without a penny. Too bad, Roger had said – she had had her fingers burnt, and that was just too bad. She had slammed the receiver down when he disconnected the call and desperately cast around for some way out of the mess in which she had suddenly found herself. But whichever way she turned, there was no way out. When David urged her to bring in the police, she had shaken her head and said it was impossible. Although she hated Roger Carlyle, she was not silly enough to make an enemy of him – which, looking back now, was something of a laugh because now his only son was dead and he wouldn't rest until, in one way or another, he had evened the score.

She had made one last appeal to Luke. She had gone to his flat that night to talk to him, to bring matters out into the open and try to make him see reason. It had been after midnight and Luke, who had been asleep, was in an irritable mood. He had protested, but she had been adamant; she had come to explain a few things, she had told him. Reluctantly, he had allowed her into the flat. As she spoke, mustering all the sincerity she could, he had stood there in his pyjamas and dressing gown, his arms folded and his face expressionless. Patricia remembered the conversation, if that was what it was, very clearly.

'I admit, at the beginning, I did do a business deal with your father,' she had begun. 'I took you on because he wanted me to.' She had held his stare for a moment; he simply had to believe her. 'But then it changed. I realised what enormous potential you had . . . and frankly, I admired your talent and began to respect you. In fact, I wanted to tell you the truth when I gave you greater responsibility in the running of the business – which, I might add, you earned solely on your own merits. But your father wouldn't hear of it. As you well know, he's not the type of man you can push around. So . . .' she had raised her hands, then let them drop in a gesture that appealed for his understanding of the difficult situation in which she found herself . . . 'I had to go along with him.'

As he stared at her, Patricia had been unable to tell what he was thinking. His eyes had been a little puffy from the sleep she had disturbed. She had forged on. 'I don't blame you for getting back at him, and I can see from your point of view that he deserves it.' She had given him a quick conspiratorial smile. His own face had been stony. 'I know you're a decent person,' she had gone on warmly. 'I could see that when we worked together – so I can't believe you would seriously want me to be left with nothing.' She had smiled again, a little nervously. 'I can understand you would want to get back at me in some way . . . make me worry for a while. Fair enough. But I thought perhaps now you could write me a cheque and we can part as friends, no harm done. Okay?'

'No,' Luke had said flatly with a shake of his head.

She had put everything into it, and having made this appeal to the sense of decency with which she was so prepared to credit him, had really believed he would relent. But she had micalculated him. Patricia's face had hardened as he continued in an icy tone.

'You can beg as much as you like, Patricia, and you do it rather well, but your timing's lousy. I don't agree to anything when I'm half asleep. Besides, you're basically as conniving and dishonest as my father is.' His eyes had bored steadily into hers. 'You didn't give a damn about my feelings when you did your deal with him, so why should I give a damn about your feelings now?' As the words, so deliberately uttered, had hammered home, Patricia had felt herself losing control. 'You can stack on as much of a performance as you like,' Luke had said with a mocking edge to his voice, 'but you're not getting a single cent from me.'

And that was when she had lashed out. That was when she had really lost her temper, and with her hand raised, flung herself at him. He had raised his own hand to ward off the blow he could see coming, and in the split-second before he grabbed her wrists, her fingernails had raked the side of his face. 'That's more like it,' he had said tightly. 'This is more the real Patricia.' His grip had been tight. 'Now, are you going to leave quietly, or do I have to kick you out?'

There had been real venom in Patricia's voice as she had warned him, 'I am not going to let you get away with this!' And with every tingling fibre of her being, she had meant it. Some time later that night, Luke was murdered.

Patricia paced the cell and waited, and the longer she waited, the more frightened she became.

TWO

Her money had to be *somewhere*; *someone* had to
know where it was – and if anybody could tell
her, it had to be Jeff O'Brien. She also had a
shrewd idea that Jeff could tell her who murdered Luke Carlyle – which made it very
important to her to get a chance to talk to Jeff
alone. She knew this wouldn't be easy; the kid
was having all sorts of problems; he had even
just tried to kill himself.

The more she thought about it, the more
obvious it became. Since he had run away from
home, Jeff had been staying in Luke's flat, and
would have learnt a thing or two. It was likely
that Luke would have taken him into his confidence. From what Patricia had gathered, the
boy had looked up to Luke from the time his
mother had been Roger's housekeeper in Perth.
Patricia didn't know too much about the story,
except that when Luke had finally summoned
up his courage to escape from a father who had

become over-possessive, he had come to Melbourne to stay with the O'Briens, the Palmers' neighbours, until he was ready to stand on his own feet, and after a short and not particularly illustrious stint as a waiter, had accepted Patricia's offer of a position with her company without realising that his father, who'd had no trouble tracking him down, was behind it.

David Palmer had posted her bail, and although he had made it plain that things could still never be the same between them, had installed her in his house in the country. It was only because she had nowhere else to turn, he had told her, that he was helping her in this way. The house was primitive – there was still much work that needed to be done on it – but at least they believed she would be safe there. But that didn't mean she should become too confident that Roger Carlyle mightn't somehow stumble across her whereabouts; there still wasn't a great deal of time if she wanted to clear her name and not be forced to remain in this awful house where there were barely any amenities at all.

Which was why she arranged it with David that Mike O'Brien should come out to the house to tackle the carpentry that badly needed to be done. There was no real difficulty; Mike was a good tradesmen, and because David was often away, on the road, he couldn't work on the house as much as he would have wished.

22

Besides, Mike needed the work; he hadn't found another job since throwing up his position with Patricia's company on the heels of the blow-up over Luke's sudden, and in his eyes, unwarranted promotion over himself – and, as she told David, Patricia was feeling rather bad about that. It wouldn't be any trouble to persuade him, and of course, when he came, he would bring his son, Jeff, to help him and at the same time keep an eye on him. Jeff bore a lot of watching these days following his suicide attempt – and if Luke hadn't come back to the flat just in time, the kid would certainly have succeeded. Jeff had to be watched like a hawk if he wasn't to start drinking again. Patricia thought she would have no trouble finding a chance to talk to him alone.

The first opportunity presented itself very soon after David had driven Mike and Jeff up from Melbourne. Both father and son were uncomfortable in Patricia's presence, barely acknowledging her greeting, and when David took Mike around the back to inspect what needed to be done to that part of the building, Patricia called Jeff back with the excuse of bringing the bucket of warm water she had been using to mop the kitchen floor across to her. Jeff obviously didn't relish the thought of being alone with her, even for so short a time.

'Luke's death must have been a shock to

you,' she said when he had placed the bucket in front of her.

He grunted, and stepped back. Patricia wasn't about to let him get away so easily. 'Did you know there still hasn't been any trace of all that money he took?' She noted his tension, the sudden wariness in his eyes. 'He must have talked to you about what he planned to do with it.'

'Not really.' Nor did the brief hesitation go unnoticed.

Patricia placed the mop in the bucket and propped it against the wall. 'Personally, I'm willing to bet on an overseas bank account.' The boy was fidgety. 'And I wouldn't be surprised if he told you the number.' Her eyes were fixed on his face. His own eyes avoided hers. Of course they had been good mates. They must have talked, shared secrets, and Luke must have gloated about what he had done to Patricia. 'Did he?'

Later, she realised she almost had him at that moment. If she had pressed it a little more, had shown a little more patience than she did. . . . But her patience had run out. 'You've no right to keep it from me,' she cried angrily. 'The money was mine, not his.' The bitterness overflowed; the injustice of it was like a knife turning in her side. 'I trusted him, and he paid me back by stealing everything. You *must* tell me!'

24

'I don't have to do anything.' The boy's attitude seemed to have stiffened, and again later, when she thought about it more calmly, Patricia decided it must have been what she had said about Luke that had got to him. 'Besides, I don't know.'

'Don't *know*?' It was too much! She had sensed she had been so close, on the verge . . . 'You don't *know*?' she shouted, in quick, jerky steps closing the distance between them, and before he had time to get out of her way, grabbing him by the shoulders and shaking him vigorously. 'You *do* know!' she accused, her voice almost a shriek. 'Now tell me! The number! I want to *know*!'

And it was just this moment, as she was shaking the boy by the shoulders and shrieking at him, that David and Mike O'Brien chose to come back into the kitchen. Suddenly becoming aware of them in the doorway, watching her in astonishment, Patricia let her hands drop from Jeff's shoulders and turned to face them. She shook her head; the fire had gone out of her as quickly as it had flared. 'I'm sorry,' she murmured in embarrassment. 'I really am. I'm afraid the strain must be getting to me more than I realised.'

But Mike was already talking over her. 'I brought the kid out here to try and take his mind off things,' he said tightly.

'I said I'm sorry.'

'You always do.' Mike was angry. 'I don't think this is going to work out,' he said to Dave who was still closely watching Patricia.

'Yes, it will, mate,' David said firmly. 'It won't happen again – I promise.'

'Jeff . . .' Patricia turned to the boy who had backed away from her when she released him. 'I know you're telling the truth,' she said quickly. 'I just didn't want to believe it, that's all.'

'Yeah . . . all right.' Jeff shifted uncomfortably. He knew something – Patricia was certain of it. A little more time, a little more pressure . . .

'Why don't you look over the rest of the building?' Dave suggested to Mike. 'I'll join you in a minute.'

Mike looked doubtfully from Patricia to his son. He hesitated. 'Okay,' he said at last. 'Come on, Jeff.'

When they were alone, David moved closer to Patricia. He kept his voice low, his anger in check. 'Just another little scheme, wasn't it?'

'What do you mean?' Patricia feigned innocence.

'The idea of giving Mike a job because you felt bad about the circumstances under which he quit his job with you. You just wanted to get Jeff out here.'

'It's my money!' Patricia lowered her voice;

she spoke urgently; he had to see . . . 'And he knows where it is. I'm sure he does. If you'd seen the way he looked when I put it to him . . .'

David gripped her arm; Patricia flinched; he spoke sternly. 'Pat, will you stop it. Whether he does, or doesn't, you've still got no right hassling him.' He released her arm. 'As it happens, though, your idea about getting Mike for this job was a good one. He obviously needs the work, and I need someone I can trust to do it properly.' His eyes were narrowed, the threat in his voice unmistakable. 'So, from now on, behave yourself and keep well out of his way – or find yourself somewhere else to live.'

But despite the threat Patricia wasn't prepared to leave it at that. Jeff did know something and she was determined to find out what it was. She would wait; it wouldn't be long before another opportunity presented itself; it was just a matter of time.

At lunchtime she made a tray of sandwiches for the men and carried it onto the verandah. It was a bright, sparkling day. She could hear the sound of hammering from behind the house, Mike was already hard at work. She called Jeff's name a couple of times before he finally appeared around the side of the verandah, and she handed him the tray. Again they were alone. Patricia decided to try another, more conciliatory approach.

'Jeff . . . about before.' Her manner was apologetic, but there was a deal of calculation behind it. 'I didn't really mean to upset you.' Jeff began to protest, but she waved it away; it was no time to be side-tracked. 'It was pretty insensitive of me to say what I did about Luke – I can see that now. I know he was a friend of yours, and his death was obviously a great shock.' She smiled sadly. 'I just want you to know that I never wished that on him. Even after he cheated me, all I wanted was my money back.'

Jeff looked worn out. His drinking problem apparently stemmed from an accident during an athletic event in which he had been participating. A lot of pain, and a way to ease it. 'It was you and his father who made him a cheat,' he said sullenly. 'He never wanted to be the sort of person he turned out to be.'

Patricia shook her head. 'It's easier for you to think that . . .'

'It's true!' he broke in defiantly. 'He was my best friend.'

'That makes what he did to you much worse, doesn't it?'

Patricia knew where she was heading, but Jeff was ahead of her. 'No. And I know what you're trying to do. You want me to turn against him so I'll tell you where the money is.'

Patricia was quick. She grabbed his wrist as he

was about to turn away. Yes . . . Her heart was beginning to beat a little more quickly. 'So you admit you know?'

He struggled to free himself, but Patricia was holding him tightly. 'Let go!'

'Jeff . . .'

He stopped struggling and glared at the woman who held him. 'What I do know is that he wouldn't write you a cheque when you asked him – so I don't see why I should tell you now where it is.'

Ah. . . ! This time she didn't resist as he broke free of her, and carrying the tray of sandwiches, walked briskly away from her. Patricia stared after him, absorbing what he had just told her – and what he had said was . . . The cheque she had asked Luke to write out for her . . . She hadn't told the police anything about that. All she had told them was that there had been an argument, that she had scratched his face – which meant . . . which meant that Jeff must have seen Luke after Patricia had been there, just before he was murdered. The more she thought about it, the more obvious it became that Jeff was Luke Carlyle's murderer.

Jeff had tried to kill himself earlier that day. He had drunk himself into a stupor and turned on the gas. He had been desperate. Luke had walked out, had told him he wouldn't be coming back – but he had come back, apparently worried about the boy, perhaps alerted by some sense that something was wrong, and found Jeff only just in time. At the time Luke was murdered, Jeff was supposed to be in hospital – David reminded her of this when Patricia voiced her certainty that Jeff had murdered Luke.

'But he was there,' she insisted. She had found him in the kitchen, drinking a glass of milk. 'He knows what I argued with Luke about. That meant Jeff saw Luke after I left him.' He was listening to her now. 'And don't tell me he didn't have the motive,' she went on in growing excitement. 'As soon as Luke got his hands on my money, he told Jeff to fend for himself and took off. Jeff was bound to feel betrayed.'

David was frowning dubiously. 'After which Jeff gets drunk, switches on the gas to end it all, and lands in hospital, sick as a dog. But that doesn't stop him nipping back to the flat, killing Luke, and being back in bed before anyone misses him.' He shook his head slowly. 'It doesn't sound likely to me.'

'Stranger things have happened.' Patricia said bluntly.

'Pat . . .' He was still shaking his head; he was finding it all a little far-fetched. 'There's no way he could have done it. He was in such a bad shape that he couldn't have killed a fly, let alone his best friend.'

Patricia fought back her exasperation. 'But he *was* there that night,' she said adamantly. There was nothing that could change her mind about that. The boy had given himself away.

'The kid's a mess.' David was beginning to show his irritation. 'He's got himself confused, and you're twisting what he said to suit yourself.'

'I'm *not*.' Patricia turned to the door. The hammering had started up again behind the house. 'And I can prove it.'

'I don't want you hassling him,' David warned.

Patricia stopped and swung back to face him. 'Don't you care what happens to me?'

'Of course I do,' he said evenly. 'But you're not shoving the blame on Jeff to take the heat off yourself. So lay off – or you'll have me to deal with.'

Seething, Patricia stamped out of the kitchen into the yard. David could say what he damned well like – he could make all the threats in the world, but it wouldn't make any difference. She knew what *she* had to do, which was to get the truth out of Jeff O'Brien, to make him confess to Luke's murder so that her name might be cleared and she wouldn't have to go on continuing to fear what might happen to her once Roger Carlyle caught up with her. It wasn't David's neck that was on the block; he could be as

31

pompous as he damned well liked.

That afternoon she had an unexpected visitor. When she saw it was Charlie Bartlett who stepped out of the car she had noticed coming up the drive, Patricia was at first annoyed at the nerve of the woman, showing up like this out of the blue after the trouble she had caused, but then, seeing that Charlie was genuinely regretful for having given Patricia away to the police, and knowing Charlie for being . . . well, Charlie, she softened and actually realised how glad she was to see her. 'You'd better stick around for a while,' she suggested, which Charlie was only too happy to do now that all her earlier apprehension about how she would be received had vanished with Patricia's forgiveness.

As they were sitting down to a light lunch Patricia had hastily put together, Patricia told Charlie about Jeff. She felt much better now that she had someone with whom she could discuss it, who actually listened to her as she voiced her suspicions and didn't try to put her down. 'David simply refused to believe me,' she said.

Charlie forked-up a piece of lettuce and chewed it delicately. 'Well, it *does* sound a bit far-fetched,' she remarked. 'But then, I couldn't believe it when David asked me about those men . . .'

'What men?' Patricia was instantly alert.

Charlie raised her eyebrows across the table.

Her cool elegance seemed out of place in the old house. 'He hasn't told you?'

'What men, Charlie?' Patricia's voice was sharper. She had placed her fork on the plate and was leaning forward on the rickety chair.

The apprehension had returned to Charlie's expressive brown eyes, as if she felt the reconciliation was to be short-lived after all. 'Two men turned up at the O'Briens' asking for your address.' A jolt, a stab of fear. Patricia sat rigidly. 'They said they were working for a solicitor *I* was supposed to have hired to defend you. But I didn't know anything about. I certainly hired no solicitor.'

'Roger Carlyle hired those men,' Patricia put in quickly. Oh yes, she knew that without having to be told. He wasn't wasting any time. Patricia felt weak. 'The only way I'm going to stop Roger hounding me is to prove my innocence.'

Charlie raised her cup. She was becoming more confident again. 'Tall order.'

'Not if I make Jeff confess.' Patricia stared intently at Charlie who slowly replaced the cup in the saucer without drinking from it. 'But I'll need a witness.'

Charlie shifted awkwardly in her seat. 'Don't look at me,' she murmured.

'You owe me, Charlie,' Patricia reminded her acerbically. 'I wouldn't have been arrested in the first place if you hadn't blown my alibi.'

Charlie considered this. She frowned, she pursed her lips, her eyes moved around the room, she sighed. 'What do I have to do?' she asked in a tone of resignation.

'Just be there when I get him alone,' Patricia replied.

Charlie was still doubtful. 'Isn't there any other way?'

'No.' Patricia shook her head; there definitely wasn't any other way. 'And we can't waste time, either. Those men weren't looking for me to tell me I had won the lottery. No . . .' She stood up. 'I have to clear my name before they find me,' she said with determination.

She knew that Dave and Mike had arranged to drive out to the timber yard that afternoon to pick up some wood. The yard was about twenty kilometres away, which gave her plenty of time once she had worked out a way of making sure Jeff remained behind.

It wasn't difficult. She told them she needed wood for the stove, and while Jeff didn't like the idea of staying behind and protested that he had just pulled to pieces a wash-stand the remains of which were on the wood heap, Mike reminded him that they still needed to be chopped into kindling. Jeff had no choice but to stay. Just before he drove off with Mike, David gave Patricia a warning look. She smiled reassuringly back at him.

About an hour later, when Jeff brought a box of wood pieces into the kitchen, Patricia startled him by following him in from outside and standing between him and the back door. Her voice was steely. 'We have to talk, Jeff.'

Quickly recovering from his surprise, Jeff was on the defensive 'What about?' He put down the box of wood.

Patricia came straight to the point; there was no other way. 'Luke's murder.'

The boy froze. His eyes flickered away from her. 'I don't know anything.' He turned to leave by the door that led out onto the verandah, but just at that moment. Charlie blocked his way by appearing from the verandah and closing the door behind her. Jeff was effectively trapped; that was the way Patricia had planned it with Charlie.

'I think you do,' Patricia told him flatly. She moved closer towards him. 'And you're not leaving this room until you tell me the truth.' The boy remained silent. Charlie remained uncomfortably by the door; this sort of confrontation was just not her scene at all. Patricia steadily applied the pressure. 'If you are innocent, why didn't you tell the police Luke was alive after I left him?' A startled expression appeared in Jeff's eyes as it had apparently dawned on him that through a slip of the tongue he must have given himself away. Patricia pressed on. 'You could have cleared my name if you had spoken up. Why didn't you?'

'Because I wasn't there,' Jeff answered defiantly.

'Then why did you tell me you were?' She had him now; he had really been pushed into a corner.

'I didn't. I never said anything.'

She sprang. 'You said Luke wouldn't sign a cheque. But he and I were the only ones who knew that . . .' she smiled grimly . . . 'unless you saw him after I did.' She paused to allow this to sink in. She could see he was scared – and guilty. 'Look, Jeff,' she went on more reasonably, 'I know you're scared, but it's bound to come out sooner or later.' Her smile now was softer, more of an appeal. 'So why not do the decent thing and admit everything now? I'm sure your parents will stand by you.'

'Patricia's right,' Charlie said from her position by the verandah door. 'And I'm sure a jury will be sympathetic.'

Jeff's voice rose, became unsteady; he was beginning to panic. 'No one heard me say anything about a cheque,' he cried. 'You've got no proof.'

Patricia knew she was getting close. He was making a brave effort, but it wasn't good enough. 'I know what happened, though,' she said evenly. 'You killed Luke.'

36

'I *couldn't* have done it,' the boy persisted stubbornly. 'I was in hospital.'

Patricia had been waiting for this. 'But you got out of your hospital bed and went back to the flat, didn't you?'

'No!' Jeff almost shouted the word.

Patricia pushed home the advantage she knew was hers. She didn't take her eyes off the boy. 'You weren't feeling too good when you got there. You saw that bottle of Scotch and took a drink. You needed it to steady your nerves. Luke heard something and came out to investigate . . .'

Jeff was shaking. 'No! It wasn't like that!'

Then what? He was cracking. 'But I'm close, aren't I?' Patricia proceeded with a scenario which she hoped was close enough to the truth, and as she developed it, becoming increasingly more confident as she went along, she could see by the expression in the boy's face that she was striking close to home.

'He said something about your drinking,' she continued relentlessly. 'You tried to get him off the track by asking him how he received the scratches on his face. He told you about me, and tried to take the bottle from you. There was a struggle. You lashed out with the bottle and struck him on the head. He struck his head again as he fell. When he didn't move and you realised he was dead, you panicked and rushed back to the hospital.'

'No!' the boy had yelled, backing away from her. 'You're wrong! You're wrong!' And Patricia knew she was right.

'The irony of it all is,' she said, 'that you'd gone there to thank him for saving your life. Right?' But you never got to tell him.'

She could see in his eyes how close she was; the whole story was there in his eyes. All she had to do was get him to admit to it aloud, while Charlie was there to witness it . . .

For a long moment, Jeff just stood there, as if in a trance. Then, suddenly, snapping out of it, and catching Patricia by surprise, he swung away from her and made a dash for the door where Charlie was standing, cannoning into her before she had a chance to get out of his way, shoving her roughly to one side, wrenching open the door and rushing headlong out into the yard. By the time Patricia and Charlie had recovered themselves and followed him outside, there was the sound of an accelerating motor, a screech of tyres and a cloud of dust as Charlie's car sped down the drive and swerved widely out onto the road, almost crashing into a tree. 'Oh my God!' Charlie cried. 'He's going to kill himself!'

Which would have been just Patricia's luck. A few more minutes, and she would have had the whole story out of him. She looked around the yard. 'I need a car.'

'There isn't one,' Charlie observed.

Patricia made no attempt to hide her disappointment. She swore bitterly. 'A few more minutes, and I would have had him for sure.'

They stood together on the balcony, while the dust slowly settled. 'Perhaps he'll own up, anyway, when he's had a chance to think about it,' Charlie suggested.

Patricia was thinking hard. She had to get to a telephone; there wasn't one in the house. 'Not unless I keep pouring on the pressure,' she said, stepping down from the verandah and striding off across the yard.

'Don't see how you can,' Charlie called after her. 'Stranded out here.'

'I'm not beaten yet,' Patricia returned. 'Come on.'

Charlie stared after her uncertainly for a moment, then, with a sigh of resignation, ran to catch up with her.

It took them almost an hour to find a public telephone, by which time Jeff would have arrived home – Patricia was sure that was where he would have gone; he would feel comparatively safe there. But when she dialled the O'Briens' number, there was no reply. After a short pause, she tried again – then again; she knew her instinct was right; he would go home. Ignoring Charlie's signs of impatience, she kept dialling the number and let it ring until it was automatically cut off.

39

Finally, after about ten minutes, Patricia caught her breath as the telephone in the O'Brien house was answered and Jeff's slightly slurred voice queried, 'Patricia?'

Patricia was taken aback. 'How did you know it was me?' She nodded vaguely to a wide-eyed Charlie, who, through the glass door of the telephone box, was mouthing Jeff's name.

'I thought that's who it would be.' Patricia could tell by his voice that he had been drinking. 'I thought you would ring home and try to kick up a stink.'

'You thought right,' Patricia said drily.

'You haven't talked to them yet, have you? Mum and Dad, I mean?'

'Not yet. But I will as soon as I can – don't you worry about that.'

'Good.' Jeff sounded relieved. 'Now listen. I want to make a deal. I'll tell you where your money is if you get off my back.'

Patricia glanced out at Charlie. 'What good is money if I'm in gaol?' she countered.

'All right,' Jeff said after a brief pause. 'Just give me a couple of days . . . let me organise something . . .'

Now they were getting somewhere. 'Okay. Have you got the details there?'

'Yeah, right in front of me. I found them on a piece of paper hidden beneath the lining in one of the drawers.'

Patricia slid open the door of the telephone box. Charlie was watching her expectantly. 'Give me a pen,' Patricia commanded, snapping the fingers of her free hand. 'Quickly.'

'It's in the Banque . . .'

'Hold on, Jeff.'

Charlie was rummaging wildly in her bag, then with a sorrowful shake of her head, handed Patricia her lipstick. 'It's all I've got.'

It would have to do. 'Okay,' she said into the mouthpiece.

'Banque Nationale Suisse.' Patricia printed the letters B NAT S on the cover of the telephone book on the shelf in front of her. 'Account number three-four-six-five-seven-five,' Jeff said, and hung up before she had a chance to ask him to repeat it.

But she was sure she had it right. She tore off the cover of the telephone book and beamed triumphantly at Charlie. The number was all she needed to be able to operate the account. 'I'm halfway there, Charlie,' she said happily. 'All I have to do now is force him into confessing.'

During the long walk back to the house, the heel broke on one of Charlie's shoes. She began to limp. She was hot, dishevelled, flustered and thoroughly impatient as Patricia urged on her the importance of keeping David in the dark about the money. 'If he thought I wasn't completely dependent on him,' she said, 'he might throw me out. And while I'm here, I feel safe from Roger.'

But Charlie wasn't in the mood to appreciate the sentiment. 'Then I hope David never finds out what you did to Jeff,' she said sourly.

When they arrived back at the house, David and Mike had already returned and were unloading timber from the back of David's car which had been parked in front of the house. 'They're back,' said Patricia as they turned in through the gate and began to walk up the driveway. 'Look worried.'

'That's easy,' Charlie returned drily.

Seeing them, David hurried to meet them. 'Where have you two been?' he demanded.

'We had to get to the phone box to ring Heather O'Brien,' Charlie told him.

David tensed. 'Why?'

Patricia was facile and convincing. 'We caught Jeff pinching the brandy you brought the other night. He took off in Charlie's car. That was why we were calling his mother.'

Mike O'Brien had joined them just in time to hear this. 'He *what*?'

'You didn't say anything to upset him, did you?' David was watching Patricia suspiciously.

'Of course not,' Patricia replied calmly, but she could see that David still had his doubts.

It was Mike who diverted David's attention from Patricia by suggesting they get home to see how Jeff was. 'He's obviously not handling Luke's death as well as I thought,' he remarked sadly.

'Yeah, sure.' David moved back towards the car. 'I'll drive you.'

After they had gone, Patricia couldn't hold back her relief. She was feeling almost light-headed. As she fed more wood into the stove, and with Charlie sitting as far away from the fire as she could, fanning-herself and wondering how *anybody* could live in such a place, let alone Patricia, Patricia laughed and said, 'Oh, I can put up with it – now I know I'm not broke.'

Charlie frowned thoughtfully. 'I wonder what made the boy give you the bank name and account number in the end?' she asked.

'He's running scared,' Patricia told her, throwing another handful of wood onto the fire. 'And when the police question him again, I'm sure he'll break. Yes.' She straightened and brushed her hands together. 'And then I'll be completely off the hook – with the police, and with Roger.' She laughed again; she was feeling very happy. 'Oh Charlie, I feel as if I've had the weight of the world taken off my shoulders. Jeff O'Brien is going to save my neck.'

But her happiness lasted only as long as a visibly upset David returned from Melbourne with the grave news that Jeff O'Brien was dead. There had been a fire in the kitchen of his parent's house; his body had been discovered among the charred ruins. It wasn't known how the fire had started – an accident it would seem – but if Jeff had been drinking. . . . Perhaps he had stumbled, knocked himself out . . . no one knew at this stage what had happened. All that was known for a fact was that Jeff was dead.

Patricia was shocked and genuinely upset at the news, but at the same time the full ramifications of the boy's death were dawning on her. Now no one was going to believe that Jeff had killed Luke. He had been her last chance to prove she was innocent – and now . . . now . . . she didn't have a hope in hell.

THREE

In reality, Patricia didn't have to wait long to discover how determined Roger Carlyle was to avenge his son's murder – but as the days passed, one running smoothly and uneventfully into the other, and as life out on the property took on a dull and rather wearying routine, she tended to lose track of time which, during the daylight hours, was largely occupied by the various chores that needed to be done around the place while Dave and Mike worked hard on the renovations. She was even becoming used to the vagaries of the old wood stove on which she had to do the cooking, and the efforts demanded by the washing tub out in the laundry in which she had to wash their clothes. But hard as it was to a woman of her refined sense of comfort, at least it was safe – or so she thought.

Although she never lost sight of the fact that the danger was there, it had seemed in that short space of time to have become isolated, not really associated with her present situation, but beyond the fields that surrounded her, and over the hills, back in Melbourne whose comforts, hitherto taken for granted, she was beginning to miss with very real pangs. Perhaps she had become complacent; perhaps she really did believe they wouldn't succeed in tracking her down.

She was alone on the property that morning. Dave had already left on a run to Sydney, and wouldn't be back for a couple of days. It was still early, and Patricia had just come out of the house by the back door into the yard with a bucket of feed for the chickens. She was about halfway across the yard to the chickens when, suddenly, two men came into view from around the side of the house. She froze. She had never seen these men before – youngish, heavily built and with a definite air of menace about them, which, with the deliberate way they were advancing on her, told her that she was in danger. Then, as he raised his arm from his side, she saw that one of them was carrying a gun.

With the gun pointing at her and impelled by her fear, Patricia reacted instinctively by flinging the bucket of chicken feed at them, hoping to distract them just long enough for her to make a break for it back to the house. The bucket clattered noisily to the ground, the air was full of chicken feed. She began to run.

But she wasn't fast enough. As she swung away, the second man leapt forward and grabbing her arm, roughly pulled her back, jerking her off balance. She tried to scream, but a hand was clamped over her mouth. She was being dragged away from the house. She struggled, but it was no use; the man holding her was much too strong for her, and after a few moments she realised the pointlessness of continuing to resist.

She was bundled into the back seat of a car. The man with the gun leaned over the passenger's seat in front of her, the weapon trained levelly at her head, while the second man slid in behind the wheel. Patricia was out of breath. She was very frightened. Desperately, she tried to make a deal with her captors.

'I'll give you all the money I've got,' she gasped. 'It will be more than Roger's paying you.'

The man with the gun had cold blue eyes. 'Get down!' he snapped, gesturing curtly with the gun.

Patricia still tried. Her heart was pounding. 'Just tell me how much you want.' She was shaking. 'Please . . . let me go.'

Slowly and with the appearance that he was getting some enjoyment out of making her squirm, the man in front of her cocked the gun, and with a sinking sensation of dismay, Patricia realised there was no way she could get through to them. They wouldn't listen to her, no matter how much she offered them. She lay down on the rear seat.

As they drove, and with the gun trained on her all the time, Patricia wondered how much longer she had to live – a matter of minutes, each minute ticking away, until the final moment? Death – the last thing she would see was the barrel of the gun, and the expressionless face of the man behind it as his finger slowly squeezed the trigger. . . . She closed her eyes. The car moved smoothly along the road, the engine purred quietly. Tears of self-pity squeezed out between Patricia's eyelids and streamed down her cheeks.

She didn't know how long they had been travelling before they turned off the road onto a bumpy track and a few moments later came to a stop. Terrified, Patricia opened her eyes as the rear door was yanked open and the driver, reaching in and grabbing hold of her arm, hauled her out of the car. As she stood there unsteadily, trying to blink back the tears, and noting dimly that she was surrounded by bush, the man with the gun came around the front of the car.

'Walk!' he commanded gruffly, jerking the gun towards a clearing just off the track. 'Over there!'

Patricia tried again; she had to make them

listen. 'You have to let me speak to Roger,' she pleaded. 'Just one more call.'

The man with the gun shoved her with his free hand. 'I said walk!'

'But it's all wrong . . .' She looked from one man to the other, but she saw nothing in their faces, not a flicker of emotion. Beaten, she turned and began to move listlessly towards the clearing, expecting every step she took to be her last, waiting for the report that would be the last sound she would ever hear. She started as a hand was placed on her shoulder, stopping her. She turned. The gun was raised and aimed at her head . . .

Then through the haze of her fear, she was aware of another sound, a heavy motor starting up from somewhere nearby through the bushes. She saw the startled expression on the face of the man who was aiming the gun at her – the gun that now wavered as he turned his head – and instantly, the instinct of survival taking over before she was even hardly aware of it, Patricia was running through the bushes away from the clearing.

The branches flicked and tore at her clothing. She stumbled and righted herself. She heard a sharp crack behind her, and something thudded into a tree just to her right. In front of her, the bush was thinning out, and through the sound of her own rushing breath, she could distinguish other sounds, the flash of movement through the trees in front of her, and realised she was close to the highway. A few more yards, through the trees. . . . Something caught at her foot, and she could feel herself falling heavily into the undergrowth. As she struggled to her feet, a fierce pain shot through her leg, and became more agonising when she tried to put her weight on it. Behind her, she could hear her two captors crashing through the undergrowth. Her teeth clenched against the pain in her leg, she pulled herself behind a tree where she crouched, holding her breath, as the footsteps came closer.

The man with the gun stood beside the tree only a few feet from where she was hiding, and for a moment stared speculatively through the trees at the highway beyond. His back was to her; all he had to do was turn and he would see her. Patricia's chest was hurting from the effort of holding her breath, which at any moment, any second now, threatened to force itself free with a rush that the man on the other side of the tree couldn't help but hear. Please . . . Patricia's forehead was beaded with cold sweat, and she was certain that even over the noise of the traffic, he would hear the thudding of her heart which sounded so noisily in her own ears.

Then, to her immense relief, he was moving away, back towards the clearing. Patricia waited, still not daring to let out her breath, even gradually, a little at a time. Six yards, seven . . . another few seconds and he would be gone. Suddenly, in the tense silence, the sound of a car horn from the highway made her jump. The man turned. He saw her crouched beside the tree. He raised the gun, took aim – and once again the survival instinct took over as Patricia flung herself to one side just as the gun fired.

The adrenalin was surging, and she was hardly aware now of the pain in her knee, as with an effort she grabbed a large chunk of wood from the ground beside her and threw it with all her force at the man who was rushing towards her. The wood struck him in the chest, stopping him just long enough for Patricia to hobble as fast as she could through the trees to the highway.

Here she was still not safe; he could still fire at her through the trees. A car was coming up on the far side of the road. Frantically, she signalled it, but it sped on past. Another car was heading towards her on the near side. It *had* to stop; it was a matter of life and death. She dragged herself out onto the road, right in its path, and as it bore down on her, frantically waved both arms in a desperate bid to stop it. There was a shrill screech of tyres, and with Patricia not moving out of its way, the car swerved to the side of the road and came to a stop less than a metre from where she was standing.

'What are you trying to do, lady?' she heard a

man's voice yelling as she hurried to the passenger side of the car and pulled the door open. 'Get yourself killed?'

'Please . . .' She slid in beside the driver. 'I have to get away.'

The man began to protest. 'Hey, wait a minute!'

'Just drive!' Patricia ordered sharply. 'I'll explain later.'

He was still hesitating when the man with the gun darted out from the bushes onto the side of the road. The driver gunned the engine, and the car sped away. Looking back through the rear window, Patricia saw that the man with the gun stared after them for some moments before turning back into the bush from which he had emerged.

So it was that Ross Newman, the driver of the car, a tall, rather distinguished looking man with greying temples, who also happened to be an eminent Melbourne surgeon, entered Patricia Morrell's life – and because he had saved her life on that occasion, it was to draw him closer and closer into a net from which he was to find it increasingly more difficult to extricate as his one great weakness, gambling, was steadily played upon by Roger Carlyle who, with only the number of his car to go on, used his considerable resources to at first track him down and have him watched to find out how he might be used as a suitable tool to carry out his wishes. This was made even easier when it was established that Newman had taken it on himself to treat Patricia's knee injury, which he told her was bursitis, or inflammation of the knee tissue. In fact, it couldn't have been more perfect.

After she had been brought back to her house in Melbourne, they told their story to the police – Newman verifying Patricia's only at the point where he had seen the armed man run out onto the road just behind Patricia – who then arranged for a guard on Patricia to ensure that a similar attempt wasn't made on her. While she apologised to him for dragging him into her affairs in such an abrupt manner, Patricia was nevertheless grateful for Newman's concern. She was also anxious to return to David's place out at Sunbury.

While Newman was out fetching something for their lunch, Patricia put a call through to Perth. When Roger Carlyle's secretary told her that he was in conference, and asked if there was any message, Patricia had a warning for him. Carlyle's apes, she said, had bungled the job that morning, and now Patricia had got herself some police protection. So unless Roger wanted to end up on a charge, she said angrily before slamming the receiver down, he had better back off.

Even after he had taken her back to Sunbury,

it seemed to Patricia that, for a surgeon, Ross Newman seemed to have a great deal of spare time to lavish on her. 'Not really,' he said with a laugh when she lightly suggested this to him, 'I just think you're worthy of special treatment, that's all.' To ease the pain, he had given her injections and a bottle of tablets to take. He also made an appointment for her to have her knee X-rayed. He was paying her a great deal of attention.

By the time David Palmer returned to Sunbury, a police guard had been placed on the property and a telephone installed in case of emergency. Patricia was overjoyed to see him, and as she told him what had happened that morning after he had gone away in his truck, she almost broke down at the memory of how close she had been to death. David, reproaching himself for having left her alone, took her in his arms and comforted her, then suddenly realising how close he was to falling back into the role of a lover instead of a concerned friend, gently disengaged himself.

She introduced Ross to David, who seemed a little reserved in the doctor's presence, and after a few moments left with the excuse of having things to do around the back. Patricia thought she recognised signs of jealousy, and was pleased.

When she began to have bouts of anxiety and

depression, she put it down to a delayed reaction to everything that had happened since Luke Carlyle's murder, and no matter how hard she tried to shake it off, she was unable to do so. She was being irrational, she knew, but she couldn't help it. There were times when she thought she must be going crazy – and sometimes, catching his expression, she suspected that that was what David was also thinking. When Ross suggested she see a psychiatrist, she baulked at first. What if she really was becoming crazy? 'You'll be fine,' he reassured her. 'Please trust me.' But she still had her doubts about the outcome.

But *something* was happening to her. It was getting worse. She was having nightmares, and then there was the telephone call from her sister, Margaret – and she knew it wasn't a dream. Margaret was dead, and yet it had been her voice she had heard in that instant before she dropped the receiver and screamed for David who was chopping wood in the back yard. But if she hadn't dreamed it . . . then what? Was she really beginning to lose hold on reality? Was she really losing her mind? She remembered how, a few days earlier, she had discovered Margaret's photograph was missing from her bag. She had told Ross Newman at the time that she was certain someone had stolen it – she was sure it hadn't been mislaid as David had suggested.

The following morning, when Ross drove out

to the property to take her to her appointment with the psychiatrist, he gave Patricia an injection to calm her down. She'd had little sleep during the night, and was tense. Telling her he had some good news, he handed her Margaret's photograph. One of the nurses had found it at the hospital, he said. Patricia couldn't understand how it could have got there. She must have dropped it, he said. But she was still certain it had been stolen.

As they drove along the highway, the police car following them at some distance behind, Patricia began to feel drowsy. The glare of the sun hurt her eyes; things were becoming blurred, losing focus. She blinked in an attempt to clear her vision. Margaret's photograph was on her lap. As they rounded a bend, Ross accelerated. 'My eyes,' Patricia said indistinctly. 'Can't . . . focus.'

Ross glanced across at her. 'Wind your window down,' he suggested. 'Get some fresh air.' He reduced speed while she clumsily managed to wind down the window, and the cool air dashed against her face. 'Nerves can play funny tricks when you become too anxious about something.' He stopped the car. 'But if you relax, breathe in a few times . . .'

She was feeling a little better. She breathed deeply. Something moved against the line of bush a short distance from the road. Patricia blinked rapidly as she tried to bring it into focus. A figure coming towards her out of the bush. . . . The outline was very vague. A woman . . . The clothes, the hat. . . . God, no! Just like the photograph – exactly the same. Patricia shook her head in puzzlement. 'Margaret?' Her hand fumbled with the door handle. . . . It *was* Margaret! She couldn't see the face clearly – but she *knew*! The clothes, the way she walked . . . She struggled to open the car door. 'Margaret!' she called.

She had the door open. She tried to walk towards the figure, but her movements were uncoordinated. Her head was spinning. The figure swam in front of her. Ross caught up with her and took her arm, steadying her. 'Hey, hold on,' he said. 'What do you think you're doing?'

'Look.' Patricia was pointing. 'Over there.'

'What? Where?'

Of course he had to see her. He was looking straight at her. 'Can't you see her?' The figure had turned and was moving back into the bush. 'Margaret. She's right in front of you.' She raised her voice. 'Don't go!' she called helplessly to the receding back of the woman. She tried to move forward, but Ross was holding her back.

'Patricia, there's no one there.'

'Yes, she is.' She tried to pull free. 'Ross . . . *please*!'

But she had gone; there was nothing to show she had ever been there. Patricia stared hopelessly at the spot where the woman she was convinced was her dead sister had disappeared. Behind them, the police car pulled up. Its two occupants climbed out and began to walk uncertainly towards Patricia and Ross. 'She *was* there!' Patricia insisted tearfully. 'I saw her.'

'No, she wasn't,' Ross said firmly.

But she hadn't imagined it; the woman who had walked towards her had been very real. 'No! No!' It was almost a scream. 'I'm *not* going mad! I'm not!'

It was the opinion of the psychiatrist they visited that day that Patricia needed intensive therapy in a private hospital, but Patricia, while admitting the need for therapy of some sort, refused to go. When she overheard David telling Heather O'Brien that on Ross Newman's insistence, backed up by the psychiatrist's report, he'd had no choice but to sign the papers necessary to have her committed for treatment, she decided she had to get out of there – which she did by abstracting the head scarf and sunglasses which Heather had left lying on the kitchen table, and which disguised her sufficiently to confuse the watching police guard as she drove off in Heather's car to Tullamarine where she bought a ticket on the next plane to Sydney.

In Sydney, she went straight to Charlie Bartlett's house. Despite her flightiness and silly
chatter, Charlie would stand by her. Later that
afternoon, over coffee, they had a long and serious talk. Patricia told her about her halluci-
nations, and how they had been at their worst
just after she'd had either an injection or one of
Ross's tablets. 'Maybe I'm allergic to one of
them,' she remarked. 'Or both, for that matter.'

Charlie poured cream into her cup. 'Did you
hear Margaret on the phone?'

'Yes . . . that's right,' Patricia said thoughtfully as she tried to bring her thoughts together.
'It had to be *someone*.' The late afternoon sun
slanted in through the window of Charlie's living room. 'But then, I saw her . . .' It was all
slipping away from her again. She looked at
Charlie pleadingly. 'Charlie, maybe I did
imagine it. What if it *is* all in my mind?' She
sipped some coffee. She was trying hard to
think.

Charlie was looking closely at her. 'Now
when you saw Margaret, you thought there was
something wrong with your eyes, didn't you?
Things were a bit blurry?'

Patricia nodded. 'Yes.'

'As if you were drugged.'

'Yes.'

'And Ross was with you when you saw Margaret. But he said there was no one there.'

It was hopeless. Tears stung Patricia's eyes. Her voice wavered. 'Charlie, I *must* be going crazy . . .'

'Unless that's what Ross *wants* you to think.'

Patricia looked up sharply. 'Why would he want to do that?'

Charlie's lips stretched in a tight smile. 'Darling, I haven't the faintest,' she said. 'But it seems to me he's the one with all the opportunities. He could easily have arranged for someone to dress up like Margaret . . . you know, using that photograph.'

'No, you're wrong.' It didn't make any sense at all. Ross?

'Well, who else fits the theory?' Charlie was slowly shaking her head. 'No one. Unless you are crazy – and I don't believe that for a second.' Charlie stared at her; perhaps it did make some sense after all. 'Could Ross have had anything to do with Roger Carlyle?' Charlie asked.

'I don't know.' It was a lot to take in at once. 'But if what you're saying is right . . . he must have. Though God only knows why.'

It was arranged that Patricia stay with Charlie until she was able to think more clearly, until the drugs Ross had given her were out of her system. She had to have her wits about her before making a move. 'You're welcome to stay here, darling,' Charlie said. 'You know you're safe with me.'

Patricia's knee was still very painful. When Charlie offered to make an appointment for a doctor to look at it, she refused. It was too risky, she said, resigning herself to put up with the agony for as long as she was able.

Of course, they tried to find her. When Heather's car had been found at Tullamarine, and a plane ticket to Sydney had been purchased with Heather's credit card, which Patricia had also taken, David was certain that Patricia would have gone straight to Charlie. But when he put a call through to Charlie, she said she hadn't seen Patricia, that as far as she knew she was still in Melbourne. When Ross Newman asked him where he thought Patricia might have gone – and it really was a matter of urgency, he said – David mentioned Charlie, but reported that she had known nothing when he contacted her. Ross said he was going up to Sydney, anyway, for a medical conference, and would look in on Charlie while he was up there.

Again Charlie denied knowing where Patricia was when Ross called on her. While Patricia made herself scarce in one of the bedrooms, Charlie hadn't found it easy to equate his charm with the ruthlessness of the hired killer she believed him to be, and there was one close moment when, to her horror, seeing that Patricia had left the tablets he had given her on the coffee table when the doorbell sounded and she had made her hasty exit, managed to divert his attention long enough to scoop up the bottle and, while she was in the kitchen making coffee, empty its contents down the sink. Later, when Patricia heard about this, she was mortified. Those tablets had been the only evidence she'd had against Ross. Now she had nothing.

The visit had given her one heck of a jolt. It was obvious that they were closing in on her, that it was only a matter of time before they realised, if they hadn't already done so, that Charlie knew more than she was letting on. They would keep her under surveillance in the hope she would lead them to Patricia – and inevitably, somehow, some time, she would. Apart from the fierce pain in her knee, which was becoming steadily worse – and something would have to be done about it before much longer – and with the effect of the drugs Ross Newman had given her out of her system, she felt well enough to make her move, which she did one night while Charlie was out at a party somewhere.

After spending the remainder of that night at a city hotel, where she hadn't been able to relax for a moment, she caught the morning train to Woombai. It was like coming home again. The memories stirred; so much of her life had been bound up with Woombai, with Gordon Hamilton's property, the riding school that was now being run by Stephen Morrell, another ex-husband, who, she found, when she booked into the Reid House, was down south attending a horse sale and wouldn't be back until the following day.

It was quiet at Woombai, among the gently rolling hills, the fields and the stands of trees, but she soon realised her mistake in thinking that Roger Carlyle would not have allowed for the possibility she might choose to hide out there – and when one of her fellow guests who Patricia had put down as no one more serious than one of those women who made nuisances of themselves by forcing their company on people who didn't welcome it, pointed to Patricia's leg when she moved it and winced, and advised her to give her knee plenty of rest because she knew, she'd had bursitis herself, the alarm bells began to ring. Patricia had mentioned to nobody – nobody – that she had bursitis. Without a moment's delay, she asked Alan Pascoe, the manager, to drive back into town for the afternoon train. She had her reasons, she said, for not staying, something had just come up, and yes, she said irritably when Pascoe told her she should be going nowhere on that leg of hers, she knew that, she intended to visit that doctor in town he kept pressing on her before catching the train – and if they left now, they would have plenty of time.

Plenty of time for her – and for Roger Carlyle, once he received the message from Woombai, to deploy two of his men who, with the woman who had forced herself on Patricia back at the lodge and was now there to point her out, were waiting for her as she limped out of the doctor's surgery.

Seeing them heading purposefully towards her across the road from where they had been waiting beside a parked car, Patricia panicked. She began to run, but her injured leg held her back. The pain was intense. She glanced quickly over her shoulder. The two men were steadily gaining on her. Another few yards . . . Her leg felt as if it were on fire.

In front of her, on the pavement outside the entrance to a milk bar, was a crate of milk bottles. Patricia limped hurriedly and painfully towards it. Reaching the crate, she bent over it, and gasping with pain, she lifted it and with all her strength, hurled it through the plate glass window of the milk bar. The sound of shattering glass was deafening. People rushed out of the milk bar. Patricia's two pursuers stopped, then with a helpless glance at each other, turned and walked quickly back across the road to their car.

Patricia was surrounded. Glass was strewn all over the pavement. 'You're in trouble, lady,' someone was shouting at her. 'Big trouble. I'm calling the cops.'

Which, to Patricia, sounded like a very good idea.

She was taken back to Melbourne under

police guard. She had stopped running, and it was as if a great load had been taken from her. Roger Carlyle couldn't get at her now – and the first thing that needed to be done was that operation on her knee. David Palmer was waiting for her at the hospital. 'Thank God, you're okay,' he said feelingly when he saw her. He held her in a close embrace. His brown eyes were moist. 'I was beginning to wonder if I would ever see you again.'

'Darling.' She was so pleased to see him, so unutterably relieved. She clung to him tightly, reassured by his strength. 'I wanted to let you know where I was, but . . . you see . . . I didn't dare.'

'I know, I know,' he murmured comfortingly, stroking her hair.

They were alone in her hospital room. The operation was scheduled for the following morning. 'It was Ross Newman,' she said, sitting down on the edge of the bed. 'He tried to kill me.'

David looked at her disbelievingly. 'Look, the bloke's gone out of his way to try and help you,' he said. 'Why are you suddenly up in arms about him?'

'It's true, David,' she said earnestly. 'He's working for Roger Carlyle.'

David was there again in the morning as she was wheeled into the operating room. When she told him she was frightened, he squeezed her hand and told her he would be there when she woke up. 'I love you,' she whispered as the doors closed behind her.

She was on the operating table. Lights shone down on her; there was the muted clatter of instruments as they were prepared for the operation. 'You'll just feel a small prick on the back of your hand,' the anaesthetist told her. 'There we go.' Patricia felt cold.

She was floating . . . nothing real any more, the lights, the instruments, the nurses moving quietly and efficiently with the masks over their faces so that only their eyes were showing, the surgeon standing beside her now . . . his eyes above the mask . . . those eyes . . . 'It's all right, Patricia,' Ross Newman said quietly as the blackness descended, and there was nothing she could do except whimper, 'No . . . please . . .'

FOUR

She had never thought that the steady thrum of the aircraft's engines could sound so sweet. They had levelled off and were well over the ocean above a heavy bank of cloud. Every minute, every second – and they were pushing the Australian coastline even farther behind them. Patricia leaned her head against the back of the seat, closed her eyes and allowed the tension to ease from her body. Safe at last – it was almost impossible to believe. Even as the aircraft had been waiting on the tarmac – a short delay, it had been announced – she hadn't believed she would make it, that somehow the delay was connected with her and that at any moment someone would come to take her off the plane. She sipped the champagne the man next to her had ordered; it was an enormous luxury to be free – to be like this, in limbo, in neither one place nor the other; she wished it could just go on and on like this, sitting here by the window, above the clouds that obscured all vision of what lay beneath them, sitting next to a handsome stranger who had ordered the champagne because he had sensed her tension was caused by an ingrained fear of flying. If it could go on like this, she wouldn't need to think. But the thoughts, unbidden, did intrude.

She knew how lucky she was to be alive – even as the layers of blackness had stripped away from her, as she had swum slowly back into consciousness, everything hazy and disembodied at first, without any connecting force to reality, time and place having no meaning for her, she had known that there was a threat, that danger was very close to her. There had been a face close to her, but it had taken her some moments to bring it into focus . . . a friendly face, not handsome, but . . . steadfast. David! There had been another face, but this one had been covered by a surgical mask that left only the eyes showing . . . and that had been on the other side of the blackness . . . and then, on top of the returning fear, had come the disbelief. She was still alive! That was the amazing part.

'Believe me, there is no more exciting city in the world than Rio.' The man in the seat next to her was smiling at her over his glass. There was barely repressed energy in his expression, his movements. His English was slightly accented. 'You will love it.'

'I hope so.' Patricia suddenly thought of David. She would miss him very much. A constriction began to form in her throat. 'You've been there?' she asked.

'Many times,' he replied with a chuckle. 'I am an airline director – in Buenos Aires. My name is Roberto Quinteros.' His light brown eyes studied her enquiringly.

'Margaret,' she said simply.

'Just Margaret?'

'Yes.'

He smiled. 'I like a touch of mystery,' he said, toasting her with his glass. 'You are joining someone in Rio?'

'No. I . . . I'm leaving someone behind . . . in Australia.' The constriction was forming again. David . . . She smiled wistfully back at him, then, before he could see her tears, turned quickly away to stare through the window next to her.

'Ah . . . the end of a love affair?' He raised his glass again. 'Well . . . so . . . a new start, a new city. And a new friend to show it to you.'

David had told her what had happened – how, when he had learned that the operation was to be performed by Ross Newman, and worried by what Patricia had said about him – he hadn't wanted to take the chance, he had said – he had gone straight to the hospital superintendent, had browbeaten him, had refused to take no for an answer, until, finally, the man had agreed to look in on the operation to make sure it proceeded along uneventful lines. David had still been doubtful, though. 'If he did mean to try anything . . . you know, during the operation,' he had said, 'he would have had to make it look convincing. The other people – the anaesthetist, for instance.'

'The anaesthetist could have been bribed just as easily as Ross apparently was,' Patricia had suggested. 'Everyone has their price, after all – and Roger Carlyle will stop at nothing to get the person he thinks killed his son.'

Nor had he stopped at nothing. He was out to get her, and it didn't matter to him how many people were hurt in the process – or even killed. And when that wheelchair exploded . . . She shuddered and stared at the clouds below. By rights she should have been sitting in that chair; that was what Roger Carlyle would have expected. It would have been very simple, her hand on the lever, pushing it forward, triggering the device that had been planted there – planted on the wheelchair that had been substituted for her own by those bogus delivery men – and that would have been the end of it. A room full of people – and it was lucky, she guessed, that only one of those people had been killed, that friend of Fiona Thompson's, Barney whatsisname, who had been fiddling with the wheelchair's controls. Patricia hadn't been touched by the blast; she had been moving around the room on her walking sticks, talking to people most of whom hated her guts but had made the effort to come out to David's place for the party – Charlie Bartlett's bright idea, actually – that had been arranged with the intention of cheering her up after her operation. At the moment of the blast, she had been standing on the far side of the room, and with David standing in front of her, effectively shielding her, and she had emerged unscathed from that scene of absolute chaos, from the billowing smoke, flying plaster, and with people wandering around dazed and bleeding. All those people hurt, that man killed – just because of her. It was too awful to think about. And it wouldn't end there – it would go on and on until . . . there would be a next time, and surely her luck couldn't hold out much longer. Not unless . . . well, there was one answer. It was time she disappeared – and for good.

Only Charlie was to know about it. 'I think you're doing the wrong thing,' she had said doubtfully when Patricia let her in on the plan. 'Going overseas doesn't solve anything.'

Patricia had snapped at her; she had expected a more positive reaction from Charlie than that. 'Then you tell me what other choice I have?' Of course Charlie hadn't had an answer to that. 'If I stay,' Patricia had gone on, 'Roger is going to have me killed sooner or later. I can't be lucky *all* the time.'

'Unless he slips up and the police finally pin something on him,' Charlie had observed, which, to Patricia's way of thinking, knowing Roger Carlyle as she did, was about as likely as winning the State lottery. She had to leave the country – there was no other way.

Which had led them into the subject of a passport. Charlie had reminded her that she was still facing a murder charge, and could hardly travel on her own passport. Patricia had agreed. That was why Charlie was going to help her obtain a false one. Charlie had been horrified at doing something so illegal, but Patricia had persuaded her in the end. There was no one else she could trust, she had said. She had given the still unhappy Charlie the number of a contact she had made some years back when she had needed favours done that were not above board, and who would help her now – for a price of course.

And Charlie had come good. She had brought the brand new passport out to Sunbury, and that same evening, alone in the house with David, Patricia had been particularly sad at the thought of leaving it – and him. The house that now bore the marks of the recent explosion . . . She recalled the first time David had brought her there. She hadn't been impressed; it had too much an air about it of 'roughing it'. But in the time she had been there, and as the improvements had gradually been made, it had somehow grown

72

on her. Even the old wood stove had grown on her.

'We'll get a new one when we can afford it,' David had said that night when she told him this.

She had sighed. 'Oh . . . there's no point now.' It had come out before she could stop herself. David had looked at her sharply. 'I mean . . . I've gotten used to it,' she had said quickly.

David had seemed relieved. He had laughed softly. 'I thought you meant . . .'

'What?'

'I don't know,' he had said with a shrug. 'But the way you've been acting lately . . .' he had chosen his words . . . 'I get the feeling you might be thinking of shooting through. If the trial goes badly, that is.'

Patricia had shifted uncomfortably on the sofa. 'What makes you think that?'

'The way you've been looking at every-thing . . . almost as if you're saying goodbye.' He had reached across and taken her hand. 'I don't know. Maybe I'm imagining it.'

'You are,' she had said emphatically. 'For one thing, I'd be breaking the law if I ran away. Also, I thought you were the one who was sure I wouldn't lose.'

'You won't,' he had assured her. 'But I was still worried you were thinking of leaving.'

'I couldn't leave you,' Patricia had said sof-tly but with feeling, thoroughly hating the necessity to lie to him. 'Not after everything we've been through.'

Charlie had given her her airline tickets and money. On the excuse that she was going into the city with Charlie to buy some clothes, she knew David had been taken aback by the intensity of the farewell kiss she had given him – but she hadn't been able to help herself. 'I love you, David,' she had whispered, and he had laughed and asked her, hey, what's all this? 'I haven't told you since last night,' she had said. 'I just thought I would remind you.' She had turned away, and with tears streaming from her eyes, moved quickly away before he could see how deeply upset she was.

It had all been carefully planned. It had been quite simple to lose the two policemen who had been detailed to keep an eye on her. A city boutique, a changing room and several dresses over her arm ostensibly to try on while Charlie remained outside brightly chattering to the watch-dogs to keep their attention diverted while Patricia hurried down a side passage to the street to find a taxi to take her out to the airport. And now, after that nerve-wracking delay on the tarmac during which she tortured herself with all sorts of gruesome possibilities, she was on her way to Rio, sitting next to this handsome stranger who was sharing a bottle of champagne with her. Yes, a new city, a new name, a new life, the past now behind her, the slate wiped clean . . .

FIVE

Patricia was dead. Charlie Bartlett telephoned the news through to David Palmer from Rio de Janeiro. She had been killed in a car accident – that was what she had been told. It was a terrible shock. The body had been cremated, and through the clinic where she had discovered Patricia had been taken after the accident, Charlie was arranging to have the ashes brought back to Australia. No, there was no doubt about it, she told a shocked, uncomprehending David. She had been given Patricia's passport and a copy of her death certificate, which, together with her personal effects, would also be forwarded back to Australia. All the police in Melbourne needed to know was that someone, no one knew who, had sent the effects from Rio, and that should be sufficient.

For David, the news brought to an end a long and agonising three months of uncertainty. It meant that at least he now had something definite with which he would have to come to terms – not that it would be easy. It was just so hard to believe . . . Patricia . . . so far away, a distant country and among strangers who neither cared whether she lived or died – and that, he knew, was what Patricia had wanted most – someone to care about her. She didn't have to run away; he would have looked after her. It was all so unnecessary. Suddenly, he felt as if a whole part of his life was over.

For Charlie at least there had not been a similar period of uncertainty. She knew where Patricia had gone, had been in contact with her, was aware that she was staying with that man she had met on the plane and about whom she had been quite enthusiastic, at his estate just outside the city – and it was to this estate that she had driven in a rented car as soon as she arrived in Rio only to be told by Roberto Quinteros that, yes, Mrs Stone stayed with him for a few weeks after her arrival in Brazil, but now she had gone, alas, he didn't know where. If he could help Charlie find her, he would do all he could to help her. Charlie, always the romantic, a quality that had seen her through a few husbands and many attachments that had proved just as temporary, had been struck with the dark Latin good looks of the man, although she thought she detected a certain cruelty in the set of his mouth.

If it hadn't been for the servant woman who,

obviously frightened, had pressed a crumpled piece of paper in her hand as she was returning to the car, the trail would not have led Charlie to the clinic. The woman – Charlie recalled that Quinteros had called her Consuela when she had shown her into his study – had said in fractured English that Mrs Stone had been badly hurt, but when Charlie had asked what had happened, the woman had glanced nervously back at the house and shook her head. Charlie recalled her impression of Roberto Quinteros' latent cruelty.

At the clinic, it had taken her some time and a lot of argument to finally get to see a man who introduced himself as Doctor Santos. It was he who had told her that Patricia was dead and arranged for her to obtain a copy of the death certificate. There was nothing more Charlie could do after that but to return to Australia where the steady round of parties, love affairs and business preoccupations gradually took some of the edge off her sadness. Life had to go on, after all. However, she often did think about Patricia, recalled those cool features, the low vibrancy of her voice, and thought it was such a shame that it had had to end in such a way.

For David Palmer, too, life had to go on. Although he missed Patricia very much, he realised there was no point in moping and letting himself go as he had been doing until Charlie had broken the news from Rio. There was a lot to be done, and with a gathering will he set out to do them – and slowly, the times when he thought about Patricia, although still with a pang and regret that things couldn't have worked out differently, became less frequent. Even when he received the cheque made out to him for a small fortune and directed through a Melbourne solicitor from an overseas source, it didn't immediately occur to him that it coincided with the anniversary of his first meeting with Patricia.

At first he thought it was a mistake, that someone had got their wires crossed, but when he approached the bank on which the cheque was drawn, after not having been able to learn much from the solicitor, he discovered that the cheque had originated in Rio de Janeiro, and putting two and two together . . . was it possible? Was the sudden surge of joy he felt justified? It was then that he remembered the significance of the day on which it had been stipulated the money was to be delivered. It was too much of a coincidence, surely.

Charlie Bartlett was staying with David at the time. When he told her what he suspected about the origin of the money, she was stunned. She just couldn't believe it. David told her what was significant about the day he had received the money. 'So she must be alive,' he said happily.

Charlie was shaking her head in disbelief. 'She can't be,' she whispered.

David grinned broadly at her. 'What else could it mean?'

'I don't know.' Charlie was trying hard to come to grips with this development. 'I brought back her death certificate,' she pointed out.

'It wasn't in her name,' David reminded her.

'Of course not. She made me get her a false passport.'

'Exactly,' David said. 'She wanted to disappear completely. So . . .' he spread his hands; he was sure he was on the right track . . . 'what better way to do it than fake your own death?' It would be just like Patricia to do something like that. The old Patricia . . .

Charlie was still sceptical. 'How can you fake your own death?' she asked, following him with her eyes as he moved up and down the room, scarcely able to contain the energy he could feel coursing through him.

'Ways and means,' he replied. 'Nothing's impossible.'

Charlie was still watching him closely. When she had come down to Melbourne on some business matter to do with the fashion house in which she had a share and asked if she could stay with him because she didn't know how long that business would take, David had readily agreed. Sure, he had told her, stay as long as you like. 'But why didn't she tell me what she was up to?' Now she sounded hurt; she had always regarded herself as Patricia's best friend; there were no confidences that had been kept from each other in the past. 'I was in on everything else.' She shook her head. 'No, she must have organised the cheque before she was killed – that's the only answer. The bank has probably been holding onto it for months.'

David didn't think so. He was sure his instincts were right. He stopped in front of Charlie. 'What if she heard you were in Rio and thought . . . well, I don't know . . . maybe she thought Roger Carlyle had followed you. Maybe she was sick and tired of being on the run.'

It was a possibility Charlie had to concede. 'I suppose it *is* the sort of thing Patricia would do,' she said thoughtfully.

'*Exactly* the sort she'd do,' David said triumphantly.

The more he thought about it, the more urgent it became. David had to go to Rio himself – there were no two ways about it. But first he needed a passport, and that could take weeks. No, it wasn't good enough. He didn't intend to wait around. He had to find Patricia as soon as he could. When Charlie baulked at his suggestion that she obtain a false passport as she had done for Patricia, he put a call through to Fiona Thompson in Sydney. She also had contacts through whom she might be able to help him. She hesitated at first, but at his insistence, finally agreed to do what she could. David arranged to fly up to Sydney the following day.

In Sydney, when Fiona announced that she intended travelling with him to Rio, David refused point-blank. There was no way, he said, that she was coming, but Fiona merely smiled and said that he couldn't really stop her. 'I am over twenty-one,' she said, 'and I've always had a burning ambition to see Rio.'

They were in her apartment, facing the enormous blown up photograph of palms, white sand, surf and a coral lagoon that dominated one wall. Fiona had made tea. 'It's not going to be easy trying to find her,' David protested.

Fiona was wearing tight-fitting red slacks that were much too young for her age – although David had to admit she hadn't changed in all the time he had known her, going right back to the time when he and Patricia had first arrived in Sydney – how many years ago was it since she had taken them into her boarding house at Manly? A few more seams on her face perhaps, some lines here and there, but basically she hadn't changed. She was still the extrovert, still willing to help. Good old Fiona. 'In that case,' she said equably, 'you'll need all the help you can get. Besides, it's always nicer to travel with a friend.'

He still protested, well knowing that once she had made up her mind there was no stopping her. Finally, he had to give in. 'Well, as long as you know what you're letting yourself in for,' he said unenthusiastically.

Fiona had the appearance of the cat that had just finished all the cream. She poured more tea for them both. 'I don't mind roughing it, if we have to,' she said. 'In fact, I'm quite looking forward to it.'

Three weeks later, they found themselves winging in over the city of the Cariocas, over the great bay beyond the bastions of Sugar Loaf Mountain and the statue of Christ the Redeemer which towered more than 30 metres above the summit of the Corcovado. Below them stretched the city, hugging the edge of the bay and washing up into the valleys that were scored into the Carioca Range behind it. David stared down at the scene. Patricia was down there somewhere; all they had to do was find her.

The obvious place to start was Roberto Quinteros' estate. There was no point in wasting time. As soon as they had landed and gone through the Customs and Immigration procedures, and without even booking into a hotel, David, overriding Fiona's objections, rented a car, and following the directions Charlie had given him before they left Australia, headed out towards the estate. The traffic was heavy and erratic; horns blasted in constant and unnerving cacophony. The footpaths were crowded with people. Sunlight glanced sharply from shop windows. They passed tall, imposing buildings, and turned down wide, tree-lined avenues. It was hot; Fiona fanned herself with the magazine she had been reading on the plane. David concentrated on his driving.

A short while later, they pulled up outside the gate to the Quinteros estate where an armed guard examined them closely and asked them their business before leading them up the driveway to the house. Here, on the porch, they were met by a powerfully built man in a dark suit who introduced himself as Roberto Quinteros' secretary. Senhor Quinteros was busy, he said, and was unable to see them. After all, they had made no appointment. It was necessary to make an appointment to see Senhor Quinteros. David was losing his patience. He had come all the way from Australia to find Margaret Stone, and he wasn't prepared to be fobbed off in such an offhand way. Mrs Stone was dead, the man told him. She had died several months before. When David again demanded to see Quinteros, the secretary nodded to the security guard who was standing nearby, and whose hand now dropped to the pistol he wore in his belt in a gesture that was unmistakable. As David remarked quietly to Fiona as they were escorted back to the car, there was something quite fishy going on.

The next stop was the clinic where they saw the

other man whose name Charlie Bartlett had mentioned. Both David and Fiona noticed how Doctor Carlos Santos tensed when Margaret Stone's name was mentioned.

'Very unfortunate,' he said quickly in heavily accented English. 'Her heart was not up to the stress of major surgery.'

They were standing in the reception area of the clinic. 'You're saying she's dead?' David asked somewhat belligerently.

'Of course.' Santos blinked behind his spectacles. He looked uneasy. 'I wrote the death certificate myself.'

'Yeah, we know about the death certificate,' David remarked drily.

Santos' nervousness was suddenly replaced by anger. 'I advise you to be careful what you say, Mister . . .'

'Palmer – David Palmer.'

'Mister Palmer, I can assure you that Mrs Stone is dead.' Santos turned away. 'Now I must ask you to leave my clinic.'

But David was not ready to be brushed off so easily – not after having come such a long way. 'Couldn't I see your records, or something? Speak to some of the nurses who looked after her. Other people must have handled the body.'

The two men glared at each other. Fiona stood to one side, watching them both. 'I will not have you bothering my staff,' Santos snapped. 'You are to leave immediately or I will call the police.'

David shook his head. 'Somehow I don't think you'd like the police to be brought into this,' he warned.

Santos said something to the girl behind the reception desk. As she picked up the phone, Fiona stepped forward and took David's arm. 'We're not getting anywhere, David,' she said quietly.

David shook her hand away. 'This is the last place we know she was,' he said desperately.

'But we're only going to get ourselves thrown out,' Fiona observed.

'That's right,' Santos put in, glancing at the receptionist who was still speaking into the phone. 'The security guards will be here at any moment. I really would prefer you to leave without further trouble.'

David stared at the doctor for a long, steady moment, during which the other man averted his eyes. 'You haven't heard the last of us, mate,' he said evenly.

So far it had been a blank wall. They had nowhere else to turn – and yet, as David said to Fiona as they made their way back to the car, there had to be *someone* who could provide them with a clue as to what had happened to Patricia.

But there *was* someone, it occurred to David some time later.

Charlie had mentioned a maid at the Quinteros house – the one who had given her the address of the clinic. David swore softly. He had forgotten all about her. Fiona gave him a sad smile and pointed out that they could hardly go back to the estate and find her. There was another way, he said. He remembered that Charlie had told him the girl's name was Consuela.

It was a simple enough matter to dial the Quinteros house and ask for Consuela, although it wasn't nearly so simple, once they had gotten through to her, to persuade her to meet them that evening in a nearby alley where they would be waiting for her in the car. But she did come – and from her, piecing it together from her fractured English, that Patricia was still alive, She had been badly beaten up by Roberto Quinteros who had then arranged to have her taken to Santos' clinic for treatment. Alive – yes, she said, but different.

'How do you mean – different?' David demanded.

Consuela was sitting in the back of the car. She still looked frightened. She touched her face.

'She *looks* different?' Fiona guessed.

'Yes, yes,' Consuela replied.

There was the faint rumble of traffic from a nearby street, but it was quiet in the alley beside the high whitewashed wall where David had arranged to meet the girl. There was little light, and the air redolent with a variety of unidentifiable smells. David turned to Fiona in the front seat beside him. 'What's she on about?'

Ignoring him, Fiona was still watching the small, frightened woman in the back seat. 'Did Mrs Stone have plastic surgery?' she asked, touching her own face. 'Face doctor?'

'Yes.' Consuela nodded eagerly. 'New face.'

David groaned. Another blow. How the hell would they find Patricia now if they didn't know what she looked like? 'Is she still with Mister Quinteros?' Fiona asked the servant woman.

Consuela shook her head. 'No. She run away.'

Fiona was leaning forward. 'Do you have a photo? New face.'

'Senhor Quinteros,' Consuela said with a nod.

'He's got a photo?'

'Yes.'

Things were beginning to look up again. 'Could you get it for us?' David asked.

'No,' Consuela said in a small, frightened voice.

'Please . . . it's very urgent.'

They worked on her, pleaded and cajoled – and finally Consuela said she would fetch the photograph for them. After she had gone, the time seemed to drag. Both David and Fiona kept glancing at their watches. The Quinteros house wasn't far away; it shouldn't have taken her more than a few minutes to reach there, pick up the photograph and come back. Fifteen minutes, twenty, half an hour . . . Fiona and David looked at each other. What if something had gone wrong? What if she had been caught? Or had changed her mind at the last minute? Thirty-five minutes, forty . . . Finally, after almost an hour had passed, Fiona made the suggestion that she should return to their hotel and have a call put through to Consuela at the house. David thought that might be a good idea, and warned her to be careful.

Alone, David sat in the car, his fingers tapping impatiently on the rim of the steering wheel as he stared along the alley in the direction he expected Consuela to come – *if* she was coming, he reminded himself – when, suddenly, he was startled to hear her voice gently call his name next to him. He swung in his seat to see her looking in at him through the window. She had approached the car from behind; he hadn't heard a thing. She handed him an envelope. 'The photo,' she whispered, and before he had time to thank her, she was gone again.

Relieved, he settled back in the seat and studied the envelope for a long moment before he opened it, and began to extract the picture from inside. But before he had time to see anything more than a fringe of silver-grey hair, an expanse of forehead, and eyes that were pale, like Patricia's, the door beside him was suddenly wrenched open. He yelled as he was dragged roughly from the car, spun across the alley and slammed hard against the wall. Winded, he tried to protest. 'What . . . what's going on?' The envelope containing Patricia's photograph was forgotten. He had dropped it as he had been hauled from the car.

There were two of them, closing in on him, blocking any effort he might make to escape. He glimpsed a pair of eyes glittering cold in the dim light, the flash of teeth, a fist. He could smell the garlic on the breath of one, or both of them. 'It's time you learnt to mind your business,' he heard indistinctly as the fist thudded into his stomach – and in those few seconds before he felt himself spinning in a black and bottomless pit, he didn't feel too much pain, although he was quite certain that something had broken inside him.

SIX

From Sydney Airport, Alison Carr took a cab straight out to Charlie Bartlett's place at Dural. While she waited for the driver to take her luggage from the boot, she looked across at the Hamilton house and sighed. The acid test was yet to come. If any of them recognised her . . .

But it wasn't likely. She hardly recognised herself. That doctor Roberto had arranged to fix her up after that terrible beating he had given her – the man had turned out to be a thorough sadist – had done a good job. She had told him she wanted a new face altogether – and that was what he had done. Roberto had paid for everything.

There were lights on in Charlie's house. She rang the bell and waited in the shadows, preparing herself. She didn't think she would have any trouble convincing Charlie. She had a story all ready.

But it wasn't Charlie who opened the door. When she saw Wayne Hamilton standing in the

91

lighted hallway, she was taken aback. He was the last person she had expected to see. It looked as if that acid test was going to come sooner than she had anticipated. If her own stepson . . . or one-time stepson . . . Taking a deep breath, she moved into the light.

'Oh . . . is Charlie Bartlett home?'

Wayne was staring at her without any sign of recognition. She had to be very careful. 'Sorry,' he said. 'She's in Melbourne. I'm minding the place.' He regarded her curiously. 'Are you a friend of hers?'

So far, so good, but it was a little annoying all the same that Charlie was in Melbourne. 'An acquaintance,' she said pleasantly. 'When do you expect her back?'

Wayne shrugged. He hadn't changed a bit. 'No idea. I've got her number if you want to ring her.'

Yes, she said, she would like to do that – and did he mind if she did it from there? 'I was hoping to stay here,' she explained. 'When I met her in London she gave me an open invitation to do just that. She said that any time I was in Sydney, her house was my house.' She smiled and moved past him into the hallway. 'So I'm taking her up on her offer.' She nodded towards the bags on the porch behind her. 'Could you bring them in, please?'

Charlie's living room was exactly as she

remembered it. There was an open box of fried chicken on the table; she must have caught Wayne in the middle of his dinner. What *was* he doing here, anyway? She introduced herself as Alison Carr. She had just flown in from London, she said. Wayne was looking for Charlie's number in the teledex. Alison decided to do a little fishing; it would be the natural thing to do. 'Husband?' she asked him. 'Boyfriend?'

Wayne smiled as if at the absurdity of the idea. 'No. I used to live next door.' Of course he did. Plotting away, stuffing up people's lives. He showed her the number in the teledex. She started slightly. He was showing her David Palmer's number. 'Had a bit of a barney with the family, though,' he told her. 'So I moved in here.'

No, nothing had changed. Wayne was still being his old obnoxious self. 'That name,' she said, pointing to the teledex. 'David Palmer. I didn't realise she was staying with friends.' She hoped he hadn't noticed her reaction at seeing the name, but then Wayne was just the sort of person to observe things like that; he didn't miss much. 'Perhaps I shouldn't bother them by calling so late.'

'It's okay,' Wayne said. 'He's not there right now.'

'Oh?' She didn't want to sound too interested. 'Where is he?'

'On a holiday.'

Her performance, when she got through to Charlie, was dazzling – so much so that Charlie, after some initial puzzlement, and saying, yes, darling, the voice *was* slightly familiar, was soon believing that she was chatting to a long-lost friend from London whom she had invited to stay with her if ever she found herself in Sydney. She actually recalled the party given by a mutual friend where Alison claimed to have met her; at Alison's prompting, the details gradually came back to her. Old friends – yes, of course, and if Alison wanted to stay in the house, she was welcome to stay for as long as she liked. She was sure Wayne – 'a sweety, but, well, he does have his little ways' – wouldn't be too intrusive. As for herself, she didn't know when she would be back in Sydney. She was looking after the house of a friend of hers who had gone to Rio, and there was no telling when he would be back.

Rio? David was in Rio? Alison hoped her voice didn't betray the alarm she felt when she heard the news. There was only one reason why David would be in Rio. She felt sad. It showed just how much he must have loved her.

Perhaps it was to her advantage that Charlie hadn't been in Sydney after all. It gave her a chance to rest up after the long flight – and if she was to carry out deception with success, even to Charlie, she had to have her senses fully

94

restored. She told Charlie that she intended staying in Sydney for only a couple of nights before flying down to Melbourne. Charlie said she was looking forward to seeing her and gave her David's address. With Wayne hovering nearby, Alison made a show of laboriously writing it down.

Afterwards, and with Wayne steadily drinking, it didn't take long for Alison to realise, to her dismay, that he was showing more than just a casual interest in her – and this was some-thing she had to discourage at the outset. She invented a boyfriend back in London who she missed very much, and Wayne, taking the hint, laughingly backed off with the comment that she couldn't blame a bloke for trying. He talked about Patricia, his one-time stepmother, for-merly married to his father, Gordon Hamilton, who lived in the house next door. He said he was glad to see the back of her, and that everybody would be better off if David Palmer came back from Rio alone. But . . . why talk about Patricia? Alison was a much more interesting topic of conversation. He still suspected nothing. Alison was very careful in what she said or did. Certain mannerisms, expressions . . . Once, she raised her glass and said, 'Chin-chin.' That was funny, Wayne observed; that was an expression Patricia had always used. Alison silently rebuked herself for the slip.

As the cab approached David's house, the bitter-sweet memories came flooding back – and when Charlie opened the door it was only by a strong effort of will that she didn't yield to the temptation to hug her, so pleased was she to see her. She introduced herself, then when they were inside and settled, reached into her bag and brought out an envelope. 'Read it,' she urged. 'It's from a mutual friend.'

'From Cynthia?' Charlie took the letter. 'In London? Oh, I see – a letter of introduction. That was very thoughtful.'

'It's from Patricia Palmer.'

Looking as if she had been struck a heavy blow, Charlie listened as Alison explained to her that she had met Patricia in Rio while she was there on holiday. They had become friends. 'I don't know why she took to me,' she said ingenuously. 'Perhaps because we're similar in many ways.'

Charlie studied her briefly. 'Yes, you do vaguely remind me of her,' she said.

'I probably even picked up some of her mannerisms,' Alison said, allowing for the possibility of any future slip-ups she might make. 'I had a few problems there. She was a very good friend.'

Charlie was clearly hurt. She was confused. 'She was . . . is . . . my *best* friend!' she wailed. 'I can't get used to it. Why did she lie . . . pretend she was dead?'

Alison felt sorry for her. 'Perhaps she liked you too much to involve you any more.' It was the truth.

It was a straw, and Charlie clutched it. 'That must be it,' she said brightening. 'She hurt a lot of people – but never me.'

'She's very fond of you.' Alison pulled herself up – she mustn't allow too much warmth to show. 'That's why she wants us to work together,' she went on more matter-of-factly. 'She didn't kill Luke Carlyle, and we have to prove it. That's the only way she'll ever be able to come back to David.'

'When she sent him the money . . .' Charlie was watching her shrewdly . . . 'did she really want David to go looking for her?'

Alison thought about that; it was a question for which she didn't really know the answer. 'Probably,' she murmured. 'Subconsciously . . . who knows? At the time, it seemed to be the right thing to do . . . help him out a little.' She sighed. 'It all went wrong, though.'

It had gone wrong because David had taken it into his head to fly off to Rio to look for her, and all he had received for his troubles, as Charlie told her, was a bad beating which had put him into hospital – although, according to Fiona, who was in constant touch, he was steadily improving and should soon be out of hospital. That was something, Alison thought sadly, but it shouldn't have happened in the first place. He had tangled with Roberto Quinteros, and that had been a very dangerous thing for him to do. But David was like that . . . That was one of the reasons she loved him so much. 'In a way, you know, it's better he's not here,' Charlie said. 'He's very straight. He might have made it harder for us to do what Patricia wants.'

'Does that mean you'll help?' Alison only just managed to keep her excitement in check.

'Of course,' Charlie replied earnestly. 'I'll do anything to get her back. Anything at all.'

Alison smiled at her fondly. Dear – *dear* Charlie. She was such a good friend. Alison's heart was full almost to overflowing. Whatever people did say about her – and they said some very nasty things – it had just been shown to her once more that she was loved by those who really mattered to her.

SEVEN

It was only by sheer luck that Alison overheard those two hospital cleaners talking about a third – and thereby planting the idea in her head. All it needed was some old clothes, and a lot of nerve.

She had decided that if she was going to get anywhere in trying to prove Patricia's innocence, a likely place to start would be the hospital where Jeff O'Brien had been taken after his suicide attempt, and where, he had claimed, he had been at the time of Luke Carlyle's murder. To prove he hadn't been there . . . If there were a way of finding out, through the hospital records, who had been sharing the ward with him at the time, and following it through from there, perhaps she might learn something. Perhaps Jeff O'Brien talked in his sleep; perhaps he had been spotted leaving the hospital that night. She was sitting in the reception area of the hospital, trying to look inconspicuous but at the same time keeping her eyes open – an exploratory foray, so to speak, to spy out the lie of the land – when she overheard the two cleaners discussing a third, a woman called May who was taking a couple of days off because of the flu, which meant that for those couple of days they would have to do her share of the work as well, which wasn't fair.

The following morning, dressed in some old clothes she had picked up in a second-hand shop, Alison presented herself to the hospital reception desk and announced that she had been sent by the Hospital Staffing Agency to stand in for the cleaning woman who was off sick. She said her name was Jess Morris. She was directed to a door marked 'Cleaners', where she was told she would find everything she needed. Alison was relieved. So far, so good.

In this way, by a little judicious snooping, she managed to discover the names of the two men who had been in the ward with Jeff O'Brien the night of Luke Carlyle's murder – but they meant nothing to her. It was then that Charlie suggested they bring her son, Adam, into it. Adam was a policeman; he had contacts. He agreed to make a few enquiries when they put it to him. He was a little suspicious of Alison at first, not really understanding why she should be going to so much trouble on behalf of a woman she had met in Rio – but, in subtle ways, Alison managed to convey to him that his mother was just as involved as she was, and *she* happened to be

Patricia Hamilton's best friend.

One of Jeff O'Brien's fellow patients, he discovered, was a petty criminal who had been in and out of gaol over a number of years. At the moment he was out, and no one knew where he was. The second man was still in hospital. Alison couldn't believe her luck. Adam warned her not to be too confident that this man would remember what had happened that night; it had been more than twelve months ago, after all. But Alison was sure he would remember something. But when they reached the hospital, they were told they would be unable to see the man they were seeking. He was dying, and had been in a coma for the past two weeks. Alison's dismay was complete. They had come so close . . . Alison was in a snappy mood that night.

The process by which Charlie Bartlett, too, began to have her doubts about Alison Carr was a gradual one. Perhaps, as her son had suggested, she *was* trying too hard on Patricia's behalf – and there were other things, too, small things that nevertheless added up. For instance, the way she had her hair up one night after her shower reminded Charlie very much of Patricia. Then when she had that call from Fiona in Brazil and learned that Patricia had had cosmetic surgery that had completely changed her features, she became even more suspicious. One afternoon, while they were waiting for Adam to come up with something positive on the where-abouts of the second man who had been in the ward with Jeff O'Brien – he had a couple of leads he was following up, he had said – Charlie decided to put her growing suspicions to the test.

'You don't look too happy.' Alison looked up from the book she was reading as Charlie came into the lounge room with a worried expression.

'No, I'm not.'

Alison tensed. 'What's wrong?'

Charlie sat down heavily opposite her. 'Fiona just called. About David.'

David? What had happened to David? Now it was Alison's turn to look worried; she didn't bother to conceal it. 'And?'

Charlie shook her head helplessly. 'Bad news.'

Alison rose quickly from her chair. 'What kind of bad news?' she demanded sharply.

'I'd rather not talk about it,' Charlie said wearily.

Alison moved across to her. 'What did Fiona say?' she cried. 'What has happened?'

'Why are you getting so upset?' Charlie looked steadily up at her.

'Because if something's happened to David,' Alison snapped, 'I want to know about it!'

'But you don't even know the man,' Charlie pointed out. 'It's got nothing to do with you.'

Alison was becoming frantic; this was no time

to beat about the bush. 'For God's sake, Charlie!' Her voice was shrill. 'Tell me! What's wrong with him?'

The worried expression cleared from Charlie's face. 'Nothing,' she said.

'What?' Alison took a step backwards.

'He's fine,' Charlie said. 'It was a test.'

Alison was appalled. She had been trapped. She tried to bluff her way out of it. 'Charlie, sometimes you *do* go on,' she said with an exasperated sigh.

Charlie stood up. 'There is only one reason you would react the way you did.' She nodded. 'You are Patricia, aren't you?' she said with certainty.

There was no way she could deny it, and in a way it was a relief because it meant she would no longer have to live on a knife edge in case she gave herself away – at least now as far as Charlie was concerned. Over a cup of much-needed coffee, she told Charlie everything; she held nothing back. She described the beating she had received from Roberto Quinteros when, in a jealous rage, he had accused her of carrying on with one of his bodyguards – which simply wasn't true. 'The man was a maniac,' she said. 'He almost killed me. My face was a mess.'

When Charlie asked her why she had to pretend she was dead, she explained that she was wanted for murder, and because she thought she

103

could never come back to David, it had seemed only right to let him have his freedom. 'I was at my lowest ebb, Charlie.' She went on quietly. 'I thought I'd lost everything.' She touched her face. 'But . . . when I saw what a good job the doctor had done – and it is good, isn't it, Charlie? – I thought . . . well, I thought I could come back to Australia as a completely new person. I could try to clear my name. So . . .' she gave Charlie a rueful smile . . . 'I ran away from Roberto. He tried to find me, but I laid low for months.'

'Then you sent that money to David?' Charlie's eyes were shining; it was all so terribly sad.

Alison nodded. 'I knew he would realise it was from me. I was pretty sure he would come looking for me. You see, I wanted him out of the country before I got here.' She smiled wanly. 'He's the one person I knew I couldn't fool – even with a different face.' Not David – he knew her too well.

'I didn't know about the plastic surgery,' Charlie said. 'But when Fiona told me about it, I guessed . . . well, I thought . . . I suspected . . . I don't know.'

Alison was still smiling. 'I would have told you sooner or later.'

'But why not straightaway?'

'I was going to,' Alison replied. 'But then I

learned that your son is a policeman. I didn't want you to have to lie to him. You have to be very careful now, you know,' she added with great seriousness.

'Of course I'll be careful.' Charlie gazed fondly at the woman she regarded as her best friend even if she did have a new face. 'Oh, it's so good to have you back, Patricia,' she said feelingly.

'Not Patricia,' Alison reminded her. 'I'm Alison Carr. You have to think of me as a completely different person. Don't ever call me Patricia.' She qualified that. 'At least, not until I've proved I didn't kill Luke Carlyle.'

Charlie frowned and shook her head. 'Oh dear, that's going to be hard.'

Alison sat forward on her chair. 'Now do you see why I didn't tell you?'

'I can do it, though.' Suddenly Charlie was all brightness again. 'You're Alison. I'll forget you were ever Patricia.' She smiled warmly. 'But it's still good to have you back.'

And Alison had to agree that despite everything, it was good to be back, particularly when, with events beginning to gather momentum, she found herself back in Sydney on the trail of a lead which looked to be the most promising so far.

EIGHT

It was Charlie who had done most of the
groundwork – Charlie who, through excessive
charm worked in the right places, had managed
to track down the cab driver who was believed to
have driven Jeff O'Brien from the hospital to
Luke Carlyle's apartment and back that night –
which was all very well from the point of view of
hearsay, of course, but it was hardly proof positive. The trouble was, the taxi driver in question – one Micky Pratt, she had been told – had
last been heard of in Sydney working for Rapid
Cabs – which was something to go on, but there
was no way of knowing if the said Micky Pratt –
Charlie somehow imagined a broken nose and a
voice like gravel – was still in Sydney; people
were always moving. Still, it was worth a try.
Anyway, Charlie wanted to get back to Sydney;
she had been in Melbourne for quite long
enough. David would be coming back from
South America soon; in her last call Fiona had

told her he had all but recovered and was itching to return to Australia. Alison said she would come to Sydney with Charlie, who was overjoyed by the idea. Of course Alison would stay with her – there was no question about it. And in the meantime, Charlie would find out what she could about this Micky Pratt, who seemed to offer the last hope of proving Patricia's innocence.

Charlie was one of these people who made friends easily when she put her mind to it – and on their return to Sydney she assiduously cultivated the friendship of one of the girls who handled the radio calls for Rapid Cabs. Before long, she was able to discover that there was a driver on the company's books called Micky Pratt. After a little more persuasion, she was able to elicit the address.

The house was in Manly, about halfway up the hill on the eastern side. With no one home in the flat to which she had been directed, Charlie was walking back to the gate, checking the address on the piece of paper on which she had written it down, when a Rapid Cab pulled up in front of her. Charlie noted with some surprise that the driver, as she climbed out of the cab and came around behind it to confront her at the gate, was a woman. She tried to pass Charlie. 'Excuse me.'

Charlie stood with her hand on the gate. 'Do

you live here?' she asked hopefully.

'Yeah. Why?' The woman was short and rather stocky. She was wearing jeans and a maroon sweater.

'I'm looking for a Mister Pratt,' Charlie said. 'Do you know him?'

'I might.' The taxi-driver was regarding her with some suspicion. 'Tell me why you're looking for him first.'

Charlie hesitated. It wasn't really any of this woman's business – but on the other hand, it was vital that she find Micky Pratt, if Patricia's name was to be cleared. 'Look, my name's Charlie Bartlett,' she said, reaching into her bag for a visiting card, which she handed to the woman. 'A few years ago, in Melbourne, he picked up a boy called Jeff O'Brien in front of one of the hospitals there. He drove this boy to a block of flats, waited for some minutes after he had gone inside, then drove him back to the hospital.'

'So?' The woman was watching her narrowly.

'So it's important that Mister Pratt goes to the police and signs a statement that he saw Jeff that night.'

Now – perhaps it was at the mention of the police – the woman was downright hostile. 'There's no way I'm going near the police,' she rasped.

Charlie stared at her in amazement. 'You mean, *you're* Micky Pratt?'

The woman backed away. Obviously, she hadn't meant it to come out. 'Yeah, but you've got your wires crossed, lady,' she said, moving back around to the driver's side of the cab. 'I've never driven no cab in Melbourne.' Now she was on the defensive. Charlie followed her.

'Wait! You have to help me! Please. . . !'

Micky pulled open the cab door. Charlie grabbed her arm. 'An innocent woman could go to gaol if you don't.'

'Nick off!' Micky shouted, pulling herself free from Charlie's grip, and shoving her roughly to one side. Charlie staggered backwards and almost lost her balance. Sliding the rest of the way into the cab, Micky started the engine, and within seconds, and with a shaken Charlie staring helplessly after it, the cab was speeding down the hill. Charlie felt utterly miserable; she had just gone and ruined everything.

There was something funny about Micky Pratt's attitude, she said later to a disappointed Alison. It was as if she had something to hide. She had certainly acted very strangely. 'I really am very sorry,' Charlie said. 'If I hadn't rushed in like that, frightened her off . . .'

'We'll just have to keep trying, that's all,' Alison said resolutely. 'She can't have gone too far away.'

It wasn't until they saw the papers a couple of days later that they realised how hopeless this task might turn out to be. They also realised why Micky had been so tense.

It all had to do with a prison escape during which one man had been shot dead, while the other escapee had got clean away. It was believed that the escape had been well-planned, and that a car had been waiting at a pre-arranged spot. The dead man's fiancée, it was revealed, was a woman called Michelle Pratt, who was also missing and along with the second escapee, was now also being sought by the police. Her photograph appeared along with those of the two convicts, one now dead the other in hiding, presumably with the Michelle Pratt who, until the previous day, had worked with the Rapid Cab Company. Reading the story, Alison felt as if the bottom had fallen out of everything. So close . . . She had been daring to allow herself a small measure of hope . . . and now this. Nothing – nothing at all – had been going right for her.

'We'll never find them now,' she said miserably to Charlie. 'They're probably miles away by now. Possibly even overseas.'

'Don't give up yet, darling.' Charlie was trying to sound bright. 'Think positive.'

'Charlie . . .' Alison gave her a despairing look . . . 'if you were a criminal, would you stay around if you thought the police were on to you?'

'But I'm not, am I?' Charlie countered. 'So I wouldn't know.'

'Look, Charlie . . .' Alison was close to tears; it was all proving too much for her . . . 'I've been accused of committing a seriou.. crime. Micky Pratt is the only person who can prove my innocence. Without her testimony I could very well end up in prison.'

'I know that, darling,' Charlie said soothingly. 'I know that. We'll try and find her. Hope does spring eternal, you know.'

The following morning, alone in Charlie's house, Alison had a visitor. Charlie was down at the cab company, hoping, through her contact there, to gain a clue as to where Micky and the escaped convict, whose name, they had learned, was Ned Parker, might have gone. When Alison opened the door in response to the knocking, she was faced by a woman wearing dark glasses.

'Does Charlie Bartlett live here?' The woman was obviously nervous.

'Yes she does.' Alison was curious. 'What do you want?'

'I heard she was looking for a friend of mine, Micky Pratt.'

Ah . . . Alison experienced a surge of excitement. So the trail wasn't dead after all. 'That's right,' she said, opening the door wider and standing to one side. 'You'd better come in.'

As she ushered the visitor into Charlie's living room, Alison decided to play it cool. There was no point in frightening her away. She gestured to a chair, but the woman remained standing. She was very ill-at-ease.

'Where's Charlie?' she demanded suspiciously.

'She's not at home at the moment.'

'Then who are you?' Alison couldn't see her eyes behind the dark lenses of her glasses.

'Alison Carr.' She decided to come straight to the point. 'I'm the one who wants to talk to Micky – not Charlie.'

'Yeah?' Now the visitor was curious.

'I'm willing to pay as well,' Alison told her. She was already quite sure who her visitor was.

'How do I know you're not fronting for the cops?' The suspicion was back in her voice.

'You can trust me,' Alison said with a confiding smile. 'I have my own reasons for avoiding them.'

They faced each other in the centre of Charlie's immaculately appointed living room. 'You said you're willing to pay.'

Alison nodded. 'Yes, I am. If you're prepared to take your shades off and tell me what I want to know.'

The woman took off her dark glasses. She had given up pretending she was anyone other than Micky Pratt. 'I didn't want to take any chances out there.' She studied Alison closely. 'What's it about?'

This time, when Patricia suggested they make themselves more comfortable, she sat down on one of the chairs. 'You drove taxis in Melbourne a couple of years ago, didn't you?' It was really a statement.

Micky shrugged. 'I might have.'

Patricia sat opposite her. She leaned forward in her chair. 'Do you remember picking up a boy from outside a hospital one night? He was probably wearing pyjamas . . . maybe jeans.' Micky's face told her nothing. Alison went on. 'You took him to a block of flats and waited while he went inside. About ten minutes later he came out and you drove him back to the hospital.'

Micky had her head a little to one side as she tried to recall. 'Sounds a bit familiar,' she said, then added slyly, 'It's hard to remember so far back.'

Alison knew only too well what was on her mind. 'We'll talk about money later,' she said crisply. 'Tell me about the boy.'

Micky thought some more. 'He was a strange kid,' she said at last. 'After he came out of the flats, he was real nervous. He shook like a leaf all the way back to the hospital.'

Yes, that had to be the way it was. 'With good reason,' Alison remarked. 'He had just killed a man.'

114

'Oh.' The other woman looked startled.

'And I was blamed for it,' Alison continued. 'I'm on the run . . . just like you.' There was no harm in establishing a common bond, she thought.

'So you think my story will get you off?' Micky was watching her warily.

'I know it will,' Alison replied definitely.

Micky shook her head. 'There's no way I'm going to court.'

'There's no need to.' Alison waved this possibility airily to one side. 'All you have to do is sign a statement that you picked up a boy called Jeff O'Brien from outside the hospital, and stress his mental condition when he came out of the flats.'

'What's the fee?' Again there was the sly expression in Micky's eyes.

'Ten thousand. If I think the statement's good enough to get me off the hook.'

'Yeah . . .' Micky was thinking again. Alison could almost follow the direction her thoughts were taking. 'For twenty I will say that this Jeff paid me fifty bucks to forget I ever picked him up.'

Why not? Money was no object. 'It's a deal,' Alison said equably. 'If you write your statement now, I'll give you a cheque for twenty thousand dollars.'

The woman laughed derisively. Alison was

taken aback. 'I'm not stupid,' Micky said.
'You'll cancel the cheque as soon as I'm out of
the house. No, I want the twenty thousand in
cash. *Then* you'll get your statement.'

'It will take some time to arrange,' Alison
pointed out.

Micky stood up and donned her dark glasses.
'You've got four hours. I'll ring and fix a place
and time for the swap over.'

Alison had no choice but to agree. 'All right,'
she said with a resigning shrug.

'And if you change your mind and call the
cops,' Micky continued in a harsh tone, 'I'll tell
them you bribed me to make a statement.'

'No police – I promise,' Patricia said emphatically. 'I need that statement.'

Micky moved to the hall. 'Okay,' she said
over her shoulder. 'Four hours then.'

The tide was turning her way at last. Alison
was exultant. She called the bank, and made
arrangements to have the cash waiting for her.
From then on, it was a long and nervous wait,
pacing up and down as she waited for Micky's
call to come through. If something had gone
wrong . . . If Micky wasn't to be trusted . . .
But twenty thousand dollars was twenty
thousand dollars after all. A simple statement, a
signature. She jumped when the telephone rang.

Two hours later, she was sitting tensely on a
park bench with the case full of money beside

her. She was worried; Micky was late; anything could have happened. She might have been followed, had been captured – she had taken an enormous risk, after all. Alison scanned the faces of the passers-by. Children were making a noise in the playground across the park. Threatening clouds were building up above the city skyline. Near the lake, people were feeding pigeons. A derelict fossicked in a waste-bin. The sound of the traffic sounded far away – and above it, distantly at first, but coming closer, threaded the wail of a siren, which, if she could have but known it then, signalled the end of the brief but bloody siege in which two people perished – one of them a prison escapee, the other the woman who had harboured him.

Ashley Carter

EMBRACE THE WIND

By the bestselling author of the BLACKOAKS and FALCONHURST

Wrongly accused of murder and scorned by Mary-Stuart, the woman he loves, Jeremiah Locke leaves his Virginia home in the heat of scandal. Accompanied only by his faithful slave Cato, he heads for Spanish Florida to carry out a secret and dangerous mission for the President.

There in the steamy swamps and torch-lit army camps, he meets and falls in love with a mysterious and ravishing beauty – Yolanda Castillo Y Martiz. Yolanda is wild and spirited and she drives all thoughts of Mary-Stuart from Jeremiah's mind – for the present . . .

TESSA BARCLAY

Garland of War

Linda Thackerley is seventeen and in love. With Alan, her childhood sweetheart, now on his way to war and with the ballet.

In 1942 Linda escapes from her wartime job to tour with a ballet company, bringing the colour and spectacle of dance to towns darkened by the blackout. She discovers the excitement and the harshness of a dancer's life – and realises the intensity of her ambition.

Now she wants to go as far as her talent will take her. But how can she ever again be the shy, sweet girl Alan left behind? When he returns, how will the war have changed him? If he returns . . .

Also by Tessa Barclay

A SOWER WENT FORTH   HARVEST OF THORNS
THE STONY PLACES   THE BREADWINNER

Thomas Fleming

THE SPOILS OF WAR

'As accomplished and compelling as THE OFFICERS' WIVES and richer in scope'
Publishers Weekly

'An ambitious, perceptive and absorbing saga'
Washington Post

'The best historical fiction of the season to date'
John Barkham Reviews

Thomas Fleming

THE OFFICERS' WIVES

'If the Army wanted you to have a wife,
they would have issued one'
Old Soldier's saying

Joanna, Honor, Amy – three fresh young brides
embrace their soldier husbands in the fateful June
of 1950. As they walk beneath the ceremonial
arch of drawn sabres, their present happiness is
complete. A bare fortnight later their men are
called to war – and so begins the conflict between
duty and love, honour and happiness that is to
shape their lives … In war and in peace, across a
quarter of our century, Thomas Fleming's
epic novel tells a story of spell-binding scope
and complexity.

'Imaginative, original and
disturbingly honest'
PUBLISHERS WEEKLY

LOIS BATTLE
author of WAR BRIDES

SOUTHERN WOMEN

'Written with insight...
absorbing and convincing'
NEW YORK TIMES

'Battle, author of *WAR BRIDES*, takes on the
family saga and makes most others seem
wooden and one-dimensional in contrast . . . a
satisfying pleasure'
PUBLISHERS WEEKLY

SOUTHERN WOMEN
— three generations of women united by their
common heritage, divided by the demands of
their differing lives.

SOUTHERN WOMEN
— a rich and brilliant novel about the
enduring bonds of marriage, family and
tradition that both stifle and sustain.

Thomas Fleming

PROMISES TO KEEP

The Stapletons — a family of golden, gifted American aristocrats steeped in a history of wealth and power. For 200 years they have ruled New Jersey and the town of Hamilton. But Jim Kilpatrick, the admirer hired to write their history, cannot long be blinded to the tyranny of their past and the arrogance and decadence of the present family: the forbidding Judge Stapleton; the drunken, drug-riddled George; and the beautiful, reckless Allyn — the kind of woman that even Kilpatrick cannot resist. Together they embark on a libidinous journey, whose purpose is to bury the Stapleton myth beneath the naked truth ...

Catherine Cookson

The Garment

'A first-rate story-teller'
BOOKS AND BOOKMEN

She was young, ardent and beautiful, and she adored
her husband, not realising that his studied courtesy and
diffident affection cloaked a dull and petty mind. It
took her two years to recognise that her marriage was a
hollow sham, which could never fulfil her deepest
needs. In the restricted society of a North Country
village, affection soon turns to bitterness and sympathy
to passion. . .

This is an absorbing and moving book, written with
compassion and a sense of real concern for the moral
issues it involves.

Thomas Fleming

DREAMS OF GLORY

The wind cuts cruelly across the snowbound
landscape – it is the bitter winter of 1780, the
fifth year of the American War of Independence.
The men of George Washington's rebel army
shiver in their huts, their bellies empty, their
resentments sharper than their swords. Across
the frozen Hudson the British carouse in the
brothels of New York while their leaders scheme
to break the deadlock that threatens to bleed
the Empire dry…

DREAMS OF GLORY

is the story of two men and one beautiful woman
caught in a world of plot and counterplot,
where a night of love may be an act of treason
– and a man's ideals can fashion a noose around
his neck…

Catherine Cookson
Hannah Massey

'The story is a compelling one . . . a well-balanced, well-written novel'
BOOKS AND BOOKMEN

Hannah Massey was proud and canny. She was also intensely ambitious. In best North Country style she ruled her family with despotic power. Her ambitions centred on Rosie, her favourite daughter. She would cheerfully have sacrificed the rest of her family for her – but not even Rosie could soften her terrible, dangerous pride.

On the fringe of that raucous, brawling Massey family is Hughie – once taken in out of kindness, now ignored by everyone. But he is watching – and waiting – as the tension mounts . . .

Catherine Cookson

Cookson

Slinky Jane

'A comic, rumbustious novel'
SUNDAY EXPRESS

She arrived one morning in a decrepit old car. She
hadn't come from anywhere, she wasn't going
anywhere, so she stayed. The village hadn't seen
anything like her before, and wasn't certain whether it
wanted to. The men couldn't stop talking about her.
The ripples of her coming spread to upset everyone,
from old Grandpop Puddleton (nearly ninety) to
Johnny and Jimmy (aged seven), but her effect on young
Peter Puddleton was quite unforeseen.

'A delightful mixture of humour, pathos,
drama and near tragedy'
BIRMINGHAM MAIL

-- ORDERFORM --

GARLAND OF WAR	Tessa Barclay	£1.95
EMBRACE THE WIND	Ashley Carter	£2.25*
THE SPOILS OF WAR	Thomas Fleming	£3.95*
THE OFFICERS' WIVES	Thomas Fleming	£3.95*
PROMISES TO KEEP	Thomas Fleming	£3.25*
DREAMS OF GLORY	Thomas Fleming	£2.95*
SOUTHERN WOMEN	Lois Battle	£2.95*
THE GARMENT	Catherine Cookson	£1.95
HANNAH MASSEY	Catherine Cookson	£1.95
SLINKY JANE	Catherine Cookson	£1.95